grk:
operation
tortoise

grk

operation
tortoise

Joshua Doder

Andersen Press · London

First published in 2007 by
Andersen Press Limited,
20 Vauxhall Bridge Road, London SWIV 2SA
www.andersenpress.co.uk

Reprinted 2007, 2008

British Library Cataloguing in Publication Data available

ISBN 978 1 84270 559 9

Mixed Sources
Product group from well-managed
forests and other controlled sources
www.fsc.org Cert no. TT-COC-002227
© 1996 Forest Stewardship Council

Typeset by FiSH Books, London WC1
Printed in the UK by CPI Bookmarque, Croydon, CR0 4TD

Chapter 1

Edward Goliath was going to die.

He stared through the windscreen of his helicopter, watching the waves, a hundred metres below.

He was alone. He preferred to pilot his own helicopter. He liked the freedom that he felt inside the little buzzing machine.

Behind him, there were two more helicopters. They were flown by professional pilots and carried the people that accompanied Goliath wherever he went – his secretary, his assistant, his doctor, his nutritionist, his trainer and his bodyguards.

Edward Goliath was one of the richest and most powerful men on the planet.

But he was going to die.

The three helicopters flew across the ocean. When they reached the island, Goliath led them in a single circuit of the coastline, inspecting his property.

Goliath had bought this island for two hundred million dollars. He wanted somewhere completely private. A place where he could not be disturbed.

On the north side of the island, he had built a mansion, a harbour, two tennis courts and a massive swimming pool. He left the south side of the island untouched.

Through the windscreen, he looked down at the

beaches and the forest, the waves crashing against the rocks, the tall palm trees laden with coconuts. He liked what he saw.

When his circular tour was finished, Goliath landed his helicopter on the lawn beside the swimming pool. He unfastened his seat belt, pulled off his headset and sprang to the ground.

Goliath had a strong face with hardly any wrinkles. His eyes were blue and his teeth were white. He was lean, tanned and clean-shaven. Although he was sixty-one years old, he looked at least a decade younger.

But he was going to die.

As the other two helicopters settled on the short grass, Goliath was already hurrying towards the mansion. Several servants were waiting for him. Brushing aside their greetings, Goliath said, 'Where's Toby?'

'In the office, sir.'

'I want to see him now. In the dining room.'

'Yes, sir.' One of the servants turned and trotted towards the house.

Five minutes later, Edward Goliath was standing at the window of his dining room, overlooking the ocean.

Behind him, there was a long wooden table surrounded by twenty chairs. At one end of the table, a single place had been set for dinner. As usual, Goliath was going to eat alone.

Goliath always ate healthy food. He never deviated from the diet created for him by his nutritionist. He didn't smoke. Alcohol never passed his lips. He exercised regularly. Every day, he swam twenty lengths and jogged three miles. For a man of his age, he could hardly have been healthier.

But he was going to die.

There was a knock on the door.

Without turning round, Goliath said, 'Yes, come right in.'

Goliath spoke in a deep voice with a mild trace of a South African accent. He had been born in Johannesburg and schooled in England, then settled in California, where he married for the first time. The marriage failed after three years. Since then, Goliath had been married five more times and moved home constantly, restlessly, never staying in any particular country for more than a few weeks.

The door opened. A short, bald man walked into the room. He was wearing black trousers, a white shirt and a black silk tie. His name was Toby Connaught. He was Edward Goliath's most trusted employee and closest adviser.

Connaught said, 'You wanted to see me, sir?'

'Yes, Toby.' Goliath beckoned. 'Come here.'

Connaught walked to the window. The two men stood side by side, staring at the view.

'I read your report,' said Goliath.

'And?'

'The answer is yes.'

'It will be very expensive.'

Goliath laughed. 'Do you think I care about money?'

'It will also be illegal.'

'I don't care about that either.'

'So you want me to go ahead and authorise the operation?'

'Do it,' said Goliath. 'Do it now.'

Connaught reached into his pocket and took out a phone. He dialled a number. 'This is Toby Connaught,' he said. 'The answer is yes.'

Without waiting for a response, Connaught switched off the phone. 'They'll start work immediately, sir,' he said.

'Thank you,' said Goliath.

'My pleasure, sir,' said Connaught. 'As always.' He turned round, walked to the door and left the room.

Edward Goliath was alone. He stared out of the window, watching the sun on the water and the foam on the waves. His lips lifted in a smile. Perhaps he wasn't going to die after all.

Four hours later, another helicopter landed on the island. It was much larger and slower than Goliath's own personal helicopter.

Twelve men jumped out. Ducking to avoid the rotors, they ran towards the trees.

As the helicopter lifted into the sky, a second helicopter took its place on the grass. Twelve more men jumped out.

During the day, the helicopters flew back and forth across the ocean, ferrying men to the island. That evening, two boats arrived, carrying boxes of equipment.

The men worked hard. They hacked at the undergrowth with machetes and chainsaws. Trees toppled and crashed to the ground. Within a couple of days, they had made a clearing in the forest. By the end of the week, they had built a road and dug the first foundations.

Some of the men worked from dawn till dusk, and others worked through the night, so the construction site was never still or silent, but none of them knew why they were working. They stayed on the island for a month, then returned to their homes. Their places were taken by more workmen who, in turn, only stayed for a month before being replaced. They chopped down trees, dug holes and tunnels, built walls and ceilings and staircases, but none of them knew what they were building. They would never know.

Almost two years later, when the work was finally finished, Edward Goliath returned to the island.

He descended in the lift and walked through the long white corridors. When he reached the first cell, he peered through the bars.

The first creatures had just arrived. They were still unaccustomed to their homes. They shuffled round the walls, searching for an exit, trying to find a way to escape.

Watching them, Goliath smiled. He liked them already.

No, he didn't just like them. He loved them.

With their help, he was going to live for ever.

Chapter 2

Timothy Malt had been in paradise for thirty-six hours. During that time, he had learnt one simple fact. If you have a cold, paradise is the most boring place on earth.

Normally, Tim liked having a cold. It was a good excuse to miss school. He would spend the whole day in bed, reading a book or playing on his computer. Whenever his parents came within earshot, he would be careful to sniffle and snuffle as loudly as possible.

Having a cold in paradise was quite different.

Thirty-six hours ago, when Tim arrived in paradise, he walked down the steps from the plane, put a foot on the runway and sneezed. He looked round, surprised, wondering what had caused him to sneeze. Then he sneezed again.

His parents, Mr and Mrs Malt, walked down the steps and stood beside him. They were followed by Max Raffifi, Natascha Raffifi and Grk.

The Malts and the Raffifis lifted their faces towards the sky and smiled, feeling the warm sun on their skin. Grk scurried across the runway to the nearest wheel, lifted his leg and had a quick pee. Tim blinked, opened his mouth, wrinkled his nose and sneezed for the third time.

'Bless you,' said Natascha.

'Thanks,' said Tim.

6

'Come on, children,' said Mr Malt. 'This way! Follow me! Now, who's got the passports?'

'You have,' said Mrs Malt.

'Have I? Where?'

'In your jacket pocket.'

Mr Malt patted his jacket pocket. 'So I have.' He clapped his hands. 'Come on, children. Come on! Follow me!' He led them towards the terminal.

It was the first day of the Malts' annual holiday. They had just endured a ten-hour flight from London. Now, they were looking forward to lying on the beach, swimming in the sea, eating exotic food and doing just about nothing for a couple of weeks.

During the rest of the year, Mr and Mrs Malt devoted most of their waking hours to working, so they liked to go on holiday somewhere special. One year, they went on safari in Kenya. Another year, they went to Iceland and toured the glaciers. This year, they had come to paradise.

Chapter 3

The Malts, the Raffifis and Grk took a taxi from the airport to the hotel. Inside the taxi, Tim couldn't stop sneezing. He got through twelve hankies.

His parents thought he might have developed an allergy. Perhaps, suggested Mr Malt, he was allergic to being on holiday.

'Very funny,' said Tim and sneezed once more.

When they arrived at the Hotel Sea Shell, Mrs Malt marched Tim straight upstairs to his room, put him to bed and took his temperature. 'Oh, dear,' she said, staring at the thermometer.

Tim said, 'What?'

'Nothing,' said Mrs Malt.

'Mum. What is it?'

Mrs Malt shook the thermometer. 'You've got a slight temperature, that's all. Nothing to be worried about. Go to sleep. Maybe you're just tired from the flight.' She placed a bottle of water on his bedside table. 'Drink lots of that.'

'Yes, Mum.'

'And don't stay up reading. Go to sleep right now. Will you do that?'

'Yes, Mum.'

'Promise?'

'I promise.'

Mrs Malt kissed him on the forehead, switched off the light and left the room.

When his mother had gone, Tim drifted into a strange, disturbed sleep. He had bizarre dreams. He seemed to hear voices. He was hot. He kept waking up, wet with sweat, wondering where he was. He stared at the shadowy shapes of furniture in the room, trying to work out what had happened to his wardrobe, his desk and the posters on the walls of his bedroom. He drank the entire bottle of water and used two packets of hankies.

In the morning, Mrs Malt came to the room with a fresh bottle of water and three more packets of hankies.

Tim said, 'Can I get up now?'

'That depends,' said Mrs Malt.

'On what?'

Mrs Malt didn't answer. She felt Tim's forehead, then took his temperature. 'Oh dear,' she said, looking at the thermometer.

'What?'

'I think you're getting worse.'

'I feel much better.'

'Maybe you do, but your temperature's gone up.'

Tim fell back against the pillow and sighed.

'Don't look so sad,' said Mrs Malt. 'One day in bed isn't going to make any difference.'

'It will to me,' said Tim. He sighed again. 'It's not fair. Why did I catch cold? Why didn't anyone else?'

'Life isn't fair,' said Mrs Malt. She placed the bottle of water and the hankies on the bedside table. 'Do you have enough to read?'

'I've got three books.'

'Good.' Mrs Malt smiled. 'See you later.'

That day, Mr and Mrs Malt lay on the beach, snoozing.

9

Max and Natascha swam in the sea and did some snorkelling in preparation for their diving course. Grk ran along the sand and frolicked in the surf.

Tim stayed in bed.

He felt depressed. Through the open window, he could hear the sounds of waves splashing on the shore and people playing on the beach, laughing and shouting. He wanted to be outside. He wanted to explore the island. He wanted to swim. More than anything, he wanted to go diving in the clear blue sea, searching for sharks and turtles.

He read a book. He sneezed. He slept. He drank water. He read another book. He slept. He read and drank and sneezed and slept some more.

It was probably the most boring day of his life.

Chapter 4

That night, after supper, Max and Natascha came to visit
Tim. They stayed in the doorway, keeping a good
distance between themselves and Tim's bed, not
wanting to catch his germs. Max described the basic
techniques of snorkelling. Natascha brought a shell that
she had found on the beach. Tim didn't say much. He
just sighed occasionally.

When they had gone, Tim flopped back against the
pillow and stared at the ceiling, feeling sorry for
himself.

He had been lying like that for a long time when
someone knocked on the door. Tim didn't answer.

There was another knock on the door, a little louder
than the first. Tim still didn't answer.

The door opened a few inches. Natascha put her head
round the crack. She whispered, 'Are you awake?'

'No,' said Tim.

'But you're talking.'

'I'm talking in my sleep.'

'Oh.' Natascha waited for a minute, then said, 'Shall
I go away?'

'Do what you want,' said Tim.

He knew he was being rude, but he didn't particularly
care. The world was being rude to him.

Natascha glanced both ways along the corridor,
checking no one was coming. Then she looked at Tim

and said, 'Someone wants to see you. Can he come in?'

'Who is it?'

'Guess.'

'I don't know,' said Tim.

'Guess.'

'Dad?'

'No.'

'Max?'

'No.'

'A doctor?'

'No.'

'Oh, I don't know.' Tim sighed. This game was boring. He couldn't imagine who might have come to visit him and he didn't care either. He didn't want any visitors. He just wanted to be left alone.

Natascha said, 'Can he come in?'

'Whatever,' said Tim.

'You don't mind?'

'I don't care.'

'Fine,' said Natascha. 'Here he comes.' She opened the door a little further. A small white shape wriggled through the gap and accelerated into the room. It was Grk. His tail wagged furiously back and forth. His little pink tongue hung out of his mouth. He sprang onto the bed, sprinted along the duvet and hurled himself at Tim.

'Whaaaa...' said Tim.

That was all he managed to say before a small dog landed on top of him.

Natascha stepped into the room and closed the door behind her. She was carrying her notebook tucked under her arm. She would go to bed soon and write a journal of everything that had happened today.

For some time, no one spoke. Grk licked Tim's face. Tim wriggled and giggled and hid under the duvet. Grk jumped on Tim's head. Natascha stood beside the door with a big grin on her face.

Finally, Grk lay on the duvet and licked his paws. Tim sat up. He said, 'Does Mum know he's here?'

'Of course not,' said Natascha. 'Your mother gave specific instructions that Grk wasn't permitted in your room.'

'She'll kill you if she finds out.'

'Then she'd better not find out.'

At home, Grk had his own bed, a small basket beside the stairs. He always slept there. He wasn't allowed inside the bedrooms. Mrs Malt had decided that things should be just the same in this hotel. Grk wasn't allowed inside anyone's bedroom. Mrs Malt didn't want him getting into bad habits.

'Goodnight,' said Natascha. 'Sleep well.'

'Night,' said Tim.

Natascha closed the door.

When Natascha had gone, Grk bounded off the bed and ran round the room, sniffing the furniture, checking for old bits of food or interesting smells. He padded into the ensuite bathroom, sniffed the toilet and rolled on the bathmat. He poked his head into every corner. When he was finally convinced that the room contained no cats, mice, rats, dogs, spies, snakes, steaks, slices of ham, pieces of cheese or chicken sandwiches, he sprinted across the floor and sprang onto the bed again.

'Come here,' said Tim.

Grk padded up the bed and planted his front paws on Tim's chest.

Tim tickled Grk's ears.

Grk sniffed Tim's face.

Then Grk padded down to the end of the bed, walked three times in a circle and lay down on the duvet.

Tim switched off the light. He stretched out in the bed. He moved his feet so he could feel the shape and warmth of Grk through the duvet. He could hear Grk's breathing. He closed his eyes.

Soon, they were both asleep.

Chapter 5

On the morning of his second day in paradise, Tim decided that he wasn't going to spend another minute in bed.

He didn't feel any better than yesterday – his nose was still running and his limbs were still weak – but he was bored of being ill and tired of feeling tired. And, most importantly, he'd run out of books to read.

He rolled out of bed, discarded his pyjamas and grabbed some clothes.

Grk stood by the door, his tail wagging, his tongue hanging out of his mouth. He was impatient. He wanted to go outside and smell the new day. This was Grk's first visit to a tropical island and he was enjoying himself. The whole place was packed with unusual smells. He wanted to slalom between the palm trees and run along the beach and roll in the sand and experience everything that the island could offer.

Tim and Grk left the room and hurried down the corridor towards the lift. Tim pressed the button marked with an arrow pointing downwards. The lift arrived with a loud PING and the doors slid open.

They took the lift to the ground floor and walked through the lobby. Two big maps were pinned to the wall. Tim stopped for a minute to inspect them. One showed all the islands in the Seychelles. According to a little box of text at the bottom of the map, there were a hundred and fifteen islands altogether. The other map just showed Mahé, the island where Tim was staying. It was the biggest island in the Seychelles and the only one with an international airport. A red spot marked the location of the Hotel Sea Shell.

Tim and Grk went into the restaurant. It was packed. All the guests seemed to be having breakfast at the same time. Grk lifted his head and sniffed the air, filling his nostrils with a bewildering mixture of delicious smells – croissants and bacon, tea and toast, scrambled eggs and warm milk. He wagged his tail.

Mr and Mrs Malt were sitting at a table by the window, drinking coffee and eating watermelon. Through the window, Tim could see Max and Natascha, walking on the terrace, deep in conversation. He waved, but they didn't notice him.

When Tim reached the table, he said, 'Hi, Mum. Hi, Dad.'

'Good morning, Tim,' said Mr Malt. 'Did you sleep well?'

'Fine, thanks.'

Mrs Malt smiled at her son. 'How are you feeling? Better than yesterday?'

'Much better,' said Tim.

'Good.' Mrs Malt pressed her hand against Tim's forehead. 'You still feel a bit hot.'

'My cold has gone.'

'Are you sure?'

'Oh, yes,' said Tim. 'I'm completely better.' As soon as he uttered those words, his nose twitched and his eyes blinked. He tried to make his face stay rigid and motionless, but his muscles weren't strong enough. With a wrench which seemed to shudder through every part of his body, he sneezed.

I don't believe it, thought Tim.

'Here you go,' said Mrs Malt, pulling a tissue from her pocket. 'Have a hankie.'

'I don't need a hankie,' said Tim. 'I've stopped sneezing.' He smiled. And then he sneezed again.

'Go on,' said Mrs Malt. 'Take the hankie.'

'Yes, Mum,' said Tim. He took the hankie.

'Now blow your nose,' said Mrs Malt.

'Yes, Mum,' said Tim. He blew his nose.

Tim drank a glass of orange juice, ate a large bowl of fruit salad and swallowed three pills, determined to zap his cold with vitamins. But it didn't work. He kept sneezing. He didn't sneeze all the time, but he sneezed enough to give himself a red nose, dribbly nostrils and a slightly sore patch on his upper lip.

Mrs Malt took Tim's temperature again. It had gone down a little. She decided that he didn't have to spend the day in bed, but he shouldn't go swimming, and he certainly wasn't allowed to do the diving course.

'Why not?' said Tim.

'Because diving with a cold is dangerous.'

'Why?'

Mrs Malt looked at her husband. 'Terence?'

'Yes, dear,' said Mr Malt without looking up from his newspaper.

'Tim needs you to explain something. Why is diving with a cold so dangerous?'

Mr Malt sighed. He looked at his son. Then he looked

at his wife. Then he looked at his newspaper. Then he sighed again. 'I'm on holiday,' he said. 'Can't I be left in peace for one minute?'

Mrs Malt said, 'Just tell Tim why he can't go diving.'

'If I tell him,' said Mr Malt, 'will I be allowed to sit in peace for one minute?'

'You can sit in peace all day,' said Mrs Malt.

'Don't make promises you can't keep,' said Mr Malt. With another sigh, he put down the newspaper and picked up the guidebook. He skimmed through the sections on health and safety, then nodded. 'Listen to this,' said Mr Malt. He read a paragraph aloud. 'Diving with a cold is not merely uncomfortable, but can also be extremely dangerous. A high temperature affects your thinking and you may make bad decisions, which is always dangerous underwater. Fever increases your rate of metabolism, so you'll use up your oxygen more quickly. You may suffer spasms or suffocation. Even something as apparently innocuous as a blocked nose severely increases the chances of suffering a reverse squeeze. If you feel ill, take a day off. It's better to be safe than sorry.'

Mr Malt closed the book and looked at his son. 'There you go. Do I get some peace now?'

'Yes, Dad,' said Tim. He had no idea what a reverse squeeze might be, but it didn't sound like much fun. Perhaps his parents were right, thought Tim. Perhaps he shouldn't go diving with a cold.

Chapter 6

After breakfast, Max and Natascha collected their towels from their rooms. Natascha also fetched a book for Tim. She had brought twenty books for the two-week holiday and already read five of them. This one, she said, was the best. It was a chunky paperback called *Mansfield Park*.

Tim looked at the front cover. There was a photo of two smiling women with blonde hair and frilly white dresses. Tim said, 'It looks quite boring.'

'It's really good,' said Natascha. 'I promise.'

Max, Natascha, Tim and Grk walked down to the sea together.

A blue boat was waiting at the jetty. Two men were standing inside. Both of them were wearing ragged shorts and shirts which had been bleached by years of sunlight and salty spray. They had the faces of old men, covered with hundreds of wrinkles, but the eyes of boys, brisk and darting and energetic. One of them had a red cap perched on his head. The other was wearing a blue cap and had a stubby little cigar dangling in his mouth, curling lines of grey smoke into the air. 'Good morning, everybody,' he said. 'My name is Bish. This is my brother Percy. Welcome to our boat. What are your names, please?'

Percy ticked off Max and Natascha's names on a sheet of paper, and put a line through Tim's.

'We're waiting for three more people,' said Bish. 'And then we can sail. So, climb aboard. Make yourselves cosy.'

He held out his hand, helping Natascha leap across the gap between the wooden jetty and the blue boat.

When the other three people arrived, Bish and Percy would drive them round the island to a deserted coral reef. There, they would plunge off the side of the boat and explore the wonders of the ocean. They would wear flippers on their feet, masks over their eyes and oxygen tanks strapped to their backs. They would swim through the clear blue water, submerging ten or twenty feet under the surface, searching for sharks and turtles and all kinds of extraordinary fish.

If Tim hadn't had a cold, he would have strapped an oxygen tank on his back, attached flippers to his feet and plunged into the water from the side of the boat. He would have seen turtles and sharks and starfish and...Oh, it wasn't worth thinking about. He wouldn't see any of those exotic aquatic creatures. Instead, he would spend the day drinking fresh orange juice and sneezing into hankies, cursing the foul germ that had sneaked inside his body.

Tim stood on the jetty, watching Max and Natascha clamber aboard the boat. 'Have fun,' he said in a sad voice.

Bish lifted a hatch. Percy stowed the bags under one of the seats. Max knelt on the deck and inspected the diving equipment. Natascha turned and waved at Tim.

Tim waved back. Then he said, 'Come on, Grk. Let's go.'

Together, the boy and the dog walked slowly back to the hotel.

Chapter 7

Tim stood in the lobby of the Hotel Sea Shell and stared at the two maps pinned to the wall. He found the hotel on the map of Mahé. He noticed a path which led away from the hotel and followed the coast, leading to all kinds of small coves and hidden beaches. They looked fun. He decided to find a secret beach and sit there till lunchtime. He could sit alone and read the book that Natascha had lent him.

He read the back cover of *Mansfield Park*. It sounded as boring as it looked. Oh, well. He'd read the first few pages and see what happened. If there were any good explosions or car chases, he would keep reading.

He left the hotel and walked along the beach, searching for a nice place to sit. Grk ran ahead, sniffing the sand, stopping every few paces to have a quick pee.

Tim could imagine exactly what he was looking for. He wanted a little beach of his own, where he didn't have to watch other kids running into the surf, dancing through the waves, giggling and splashing. Where he couldn't see a single snorkel or any pairs of flippers. And, most importantly, where he could cough, sniffle and sneeze in peace.

Out of sight of his parents, he could have paddled in the surf or even gone for a quick swim, but he didn't want to do anything that might aggravate his cold. If he took things easy today, perhaps his cold would disappear overnight and he could go diving tomorrow with the others.

At the end of the beach, there was a clump of rocks and a patch of palm trees. Tim and Grk clambered over the rocks.

On the other side, Tim found a small, private beach. It was empty. Waves rolled in from the sea. The wet sand glistened in the sunshine. A large black rock squatted in the centre of the beach.

People who stayed in the Hotel Sea Shell were too lazy to walk for more than a minute or two. They couldn't even be bothered to stroll to the end of the beach and clamber across the rocks. If they had, they could have had an entire beach to themselves.

No, not quite to themselves. There was one person on the beach. It wasn't empty after all. Coming closer, Tim could see that the rock was actually a person. A solitary swimmer was lying on the sand, just beside the water, the waves washing his feet and legs. From here, the swimmer looked completely naked, but he was probably wearing a pair of those skimpy trunks which hardly covered your private parts.

Tim decided to keep walking. He didn't want to share the beach with anyone.

While Tim walked on, Grk lingered on the sand, staring at the beach and the solitary swimmer. Grk sniffed the air a few times and barked. Then he barked again, louder.

Tim turned round. 'Come on,' he said. 'Let's go.'

Grk darted in the opposite direction, his tail wagging.

'We can play a game,' said Tim. 'But not here. Let's find a different beach.'

Grk barked and ran in a circle on the sand.

Tim clapped his hands. 'Come on, Grk! Let's go!' He turned round and started walking. After a few paces, he stopped to check that Grk was following him.

Grk hadn't moved. He was standing still, turning his head excitedly from side to side, looking from Tim to the swimmer, then back to Tim again. He barked twice, loudly.

'Not now,' said Tim. 'We'll play a game later.'

Grk barked again, even louder.

'No,' said Tim. He wagged his finger at Grk. 'No barking! Bad dog!'

Grk barked again.

Tim sighed. Some people had dogs which behaved perfectly. When they were told to sit, they sat. When they were told to lie down, they lay down. When they were told to fetch, they fetched.

Not Grk. Oh, no. He just did what he wanted.

Right now, he was running in little circles on the sand and yapping. Whoah! Whoah! Whoah-whoah-whoah!

'I don't like this beach,' said Tim. 'I'd rather find another. Is that so terrible?'

Grk ran towards the swimmer, then ran back again. He made the same movement three times. Then he stood on the sand, put his head on one side and looked at Tim.

Tim said, 'You want me to talk to him?'

Grk didn't reply. He just kept staring at Tim.

Tim said, 'But what if he doesn't want to talk to me? What if he doesn't want to be disturbed?'

Again, Grk made no reply.

'Fine,' said Tim. 'Let's go and talk to him. And when

he's not happy about it, we'll know who to blame.'

Tim followed Grk down to the beach. They walked across the soft sand, leaving a trail of footprints and paw prints.

Tim noticed something interesting. There weren't any other footprints on the sand. Or paw prints. Or prints of any sort. The swimmer couldn't have walked to the beach. He must have come from the sea, swimming down the coast. That's why he didn't have a towel or a pile of clothes.

Tim glanced at the waves. There was a strong swell. You'd have to be a confident swimmer to get through those waves.

As they came closer, Tim noticed something else which surprised him. The swimmer's arms and legs were spread out in peculiar directions. When most people sunbathe, they lie on their back or their front, exposing the maximum possible area of their body to the sunlight. They relax completely. But this man looked quite different. One arm was wrapped behind his head and his body seemed to be twisted in an odd position, as if he was deliberately making himself uncomfortable. Perhaps he was doing yoga.

Tim's mum sometimes did yoga and it always looked extremely uncomfortable. According to Mrs Malt, yoga stretched the body and the mind, making you into a better person both mentally and physically. Perhaps this man felt the same way.

Tim quickened his pace. There was something odd about the swimmer. Something which didn't feel quite right. Even when Mrs Malt was doing yoga, she never looked that uncomfortable.

Grk ran ahead, pausing every few paces and waiting for Tim to catch up.

When they reached the sea, Tim realised that the man definitely wasn't sunbathing or doing yoga. He hadn't swum to this beach from one of the posh hotels further down the coast. He must have been washed ashore. Perhaps he was dead.

Tim threw himself down on the sand and looked at the man's face. He could see immediately that the man was still alive, but only just.

The man slowly turned his head to look at Tim. His pupils flickered. His mouth moved. He was trying to talk.

It was impossible to hear what he was saying. The waves were too loud and the man was speaking too quietly.

'I can't understand,' said Tim. He was kneeling on the wet sand, leaning forwards. His trainers and shorts were soaked, but he didn't even notice.

The man whispered again.

'Don't talk,' said Tim. 'Save your strength. I'll get help.'

As Tim moved to stand up, the man reached out and grabbed Tim's wrist. His grip was surprisingly strong. His lips moved again. This time, he managed to make a sound. He spoke in English with a strong accent. 'Help them,' he whispered.

'I'm going to get help,' said Tim. 'Don't worry, you'll be fine. I'll get an ambulance. I'll find a doctor.'

'Help them,' the man whispered again. Every word he spoke was quieter than the last. 'You have to help them.' His voice was now so weak that it was almost impossible to hear or understand exactly what he was saying.

'Don't move,' said Tim. 'Don't try to speak.'

The man moved his mouth again, whispering something else, but his voice was too quiet to be heard. Perhaps he was saying one word or perhaps he was saying several. His lips moved but no sound emerged.

'I can't understand,' said Tim.

The man whispered again.

Tim shook his head. 'I don't know what you're saying. But save your strength. Don't try to talk.'

The man gathered all his strength and whispered once more. This time, he spoke a little louder, but he was still incomprehensible. He said a word which Tim couldn't understand. The word was something like 'crystal' or 'collapse', although it wasn't quite either of those.

'I'll fetch help,' said Tim. 'Everything's going to be okay.'

The man stared into Tim's eyes. His arms shook. He took a long breath, as if he was gathering the deepest reserves of his strength, and he whispered the same word again.

'I don't know what you're saying,' said Tim. 'What are you trying to say? Collapse? Crystal? Cluster?'

The man's lips trembled. His arms shook.

Tim said, 'Is that right? Cluster?'

The man opened his mouth, straining desperately, trying to summon the strength to speak.

Before the man could make a sound, the strength went out of his body. His head dropped back onto the sand. His fingers relaxed, freeing Tim's wrist, and his arms flopped down.

His eyes rolled in their sockets, then stared blankly at the sky. He lay there, not moving, not breathing, showing no signs of life.

Tim crouched on the sand, staring at the man, wondering if he was dead or alive, and trying to decide what was the best thing to do. Should he run for help? Or try to do something himself? But what could he do? How do you save a drowned man? How do you get breath into his lungs?

Tim had seen people on TV doing mouth-to-mouth resuscitation. He had seen doctors pushing down on a patient's chest. He had seen drowned men sit up, coughing water from their lungs, and gasp for breath.

But that was on TV. This was here and now.

Last term, everyone in Tim's school had been offered the opportunity to do a first aid course.

Tim wasn't interested in first aid. He didn't want to waste a whole Saturday afternoon in a classroom when he could have been at home, playing on his computer. So he had said no.

And now he didn't have a clue what to do. He didn't know how to save a man's life.

Chapter 8

All along the beach, people were lying on towels and loungers. They wore skimpy bikinis and tiny trunks, exposing as much flesh as possible. Some of them, the ones who had been on the island for a few days already, were dark brown. Others were bright pink. They had just arrived yesterday or the day before, and their flesh had not yet adjusted to the fierce heat.

A sudden noise disturbed the peace. It was the sound of a boy. He was down at the far end of the beach. He seemed to be shouting something.

One of the sunbathers turned to her neighbour and said, 'Listen to that racket! It's terrible. Parents today have no control over their children.'

'You're so right,' replied her neighbour, a fat woman stretched full-length on a blue towel. 'I went to a wonderful hotel in Switzerland. No children allowed.'

'That must have been lovely.'

'Oh, it was perfect. So quiet and peaceful. Do you know, I think that was probably the best holiday of my entire life.'

'What was the name of the hotel?'

The fat woman opened her mouth to answer, but no words came out. She was staring down the beach at a small boy. He was running along the sand, waving his arms and shouting at the top of his voice. 'Look at that!' said the fat woman, pointing at the boy. 'Listen to him!'

'It's outrageous. Doesn't he know we're trying to relax?'

'Some people are so inconsiderate. That boy should be arrested for disturbing the peace.'

'And his parents. They should all be banned from the island. This is supposed to be a resort, not a playground. Why can't people learn to control their children?'

Tim sprinted past the lines of sunbathing holiday-makers. None of them offered to help or asked what was wrong. Most of them didn't even lift their heads.

He reached the hotel. On the terrace, a waiter in a white shirt was carrying a tray of drinks. The waiter looked at Tim. 'Good morning, sir. Have you been jogging?'

Tim shook his head. Sweat tripped down his scarlet face. His lungs hurt. He gasped for breath. He couldn't speak.

The waiter said, 'Can I get you a glass of water?'

'No, no,' said Tim. 'Police!' He was panting so much that he could hardly speak and the word came out more like 'puh-lease'.

The waiter smiled, thinking that Tim had said 'please'. He said, 'If you don't want water, how about a nice glass of orange juice?'

'Police,' said Tim. He took a deep breath. 'Get the police! Get an ambulance!' He stretched out his arm and pointed down the beach. 'That man is going to die.'

The waiter stared at Tim for a moment, too surprised to move or speak. Then he turned and rushed into the hotel.

*

While the waiter rang for an ambulance, Paolo Poulet hurried along the beach, stopping to ask a question of every holiday-maker.

Paolo Poulet was the manager of the Hotel Sea Shell. He apologised to the sunbathers for disturbing their peace and asked if anyone happened to be a doctor.

He found two surgeons, a French man and a German woman, each separately holidaying with their families. Neither of them had any medical equipment – they were just wearing their swimming costumes – but they both immediately agreed to help.

All three followed Tim and Grk along the beach. They clambered over the rocks. When the two doctors saw the drowned man lying on the sand, they broke into a run.

The man had not moved. The doctors crouched beside him. They took turns to push down on his chest and breathe into his mouth.

Tim, Grk and Paolo Poulet stood a few feet away, watching the doctors. Tim bit his fingernail. Paolo Poulet paced nervously up and down the sand. Grk lay down and put his head on his paws.

After a few minutes, the two doctors glanced at one another, then looked at Paolo Poulet. One of the doctors shook her head. The other said, 'We'd better just wait for the police.'

Chapter 9

A crowd gathered. Six policemen stood at intervals along the beach, holding a rope between them, making a barrier to keep people back.

Tourists stood on tiptoes and strained to see. They pestered the policemen with questions in several different languages, demanding to know what had happened.

'Hey, pal! What's going on? Who died?'

'Cosa succede? Chi è morto?'

'Qu'est-ce qu'il se passe ici? Qui est mort?'

'Was ist hier los? Hat sich jemand verletzt? Stimmt das mit der riesigen Qualle?'

The policemen smiled politely at all the tourists, but didn't respond to their questions.

Word had travelled quickly down the beach. Sunbathers leaped from their loungers, discarded their books and bottles of suntan lotion, and scurried along the beach, hoping to catch a glimpse of a real dead body.

Every minute, the crowd grew larger. People pushed and jostled. Rumours spread. When no one knows anything, people will say anything. As each rumour spread around the crowd, moving from mouth to mouth, the facts grew wilder and more ridiculous. Some said a man had been mauled by a great white shark. Others claimed a woman was fighting for her life after a collision with a speedboat. According to one of the tourists, a murderous turtle had bitten clean through a child's leg. According to another, a giant jellyfish was on the loose, attacking random swimmers, and one of its victims had washed ashore, horribly maimed.

All the tourists were enjoying themselves. Until now, their holidays had been a bit boring. They had sat on the beach, soaked up the sun and swum in the sea. It had been perfectly enjoyable, but what they really wanted was a bit of excitement. A murderous turtle or a bloodthirsty shark – that was better! That would give them something to talk about when they got back home! They strained forwards, hoping to catch a glimpse of blood or snatch a photo of the giant jellyfish.

At the edge of the beach, there were three people who didn't seem to be enjoying themselves. While everyone else chattered with excitement, these three looked gloomy and depressed.

The first of them was a small boy.

Tim sat on a rock, facing away from the crowd. He wasn't interested in discussing what had happened. He didn't want to know any ghoulish details or share any shocking rumours. There was nothing in the world that he wanted less than catching another glimpse of that body.

Tim felt terrible. He had failed. Because of him, a man had died.

If he had spent a Saturday afternoon doing a first aid course, rather than sitting at home, playing a game on his computer, he would have known how to save a life. That man might still be alive.

The second depressed person was Mrs Malt. She stood beside her son, stroking his hair with her right hand. She was worried about him, but she had no idea what to say or do. She didn't know how to comfort him. He had rebuffed her attempts at conversation and answered her questions with a shrug of his shoulders. So she simply stood beside Tim, stroking his hair, trying to comfort him with her presence.

The third depressed person was Paolo Poulet, the manager of the Hotel Sea Shell. He wasn't just gloomy. He was angry. In fact, he was furious.

Paolo Poulet stood with his arms folded over his chest and stared irritably at the crowd of tourists. He wanted the police to move faster. He wanted the beach to be cleared. He wanted the tourists – his tourists – to return to the hotel. He wanted them to eat in his restaurant and swim in his pool and buy souvenirs in his shop.

Dead bodies aren't good for business.

Chapter 10

For the seventh time, Tim explained what had happened. The whole episode, from seeing the body for the first time to running back towards the hotel, couldn't have taken more than five minutes. By now, Tim felt as if he'd been talking about it for five hours. He had already told his mother, his father, Paolo Poulet and three policemen. Now, he was going over the story again for another, more senior policeman.

Inspector Xavier Benedict was one of the most senior officers in the Seychelles. A mark of his importance was the fact that he wore khaki shorts and a white shirt rather than a uniform. If you met him in the street, you wouldn't even guess that he worked for the police.

But he behaved just like all the other policemen. He asked a lot of questions and jotted down Tim's answers in a notebook.

For the seventh time, Tim described wandering onto the beach and seeing the black rock, then realising that it was actually a man. He explained that he had run back to the hotel because he didn't know what else to do.

'You did the right thing,' said Inspector Benedict.

'Did I?'

'Yes. You didn't panic. You called for help. That was exactly the right thing to do.'

'But I didn't save his life,' said Tim.

'That's not your fault,' said Inspector Benedict. 'You

34

did everything you could.' Inspector Benedict turned to Mrs Malt. 'Your son is a brave and intelligent young man. You should be very proud of him.'

'I am,' said Mrs Malt. 'We all are.'

Tim said nothing. He knew that he hadn't been brave or intelligent. Quite the opposite. He felt like a fool and a coward. If only he had known how to do first aid, he could have saved the man's life.

Mrs Malt said, 'Can I ask you a question?'

'Of course,' said the Inspector.

'Do you know who he was?'

'No,' said Inspector Benedict. 'And we will probably never know.'

'Why not?'

'He is not the first person to be washed ashore on our beaches. It happens every few months. We almost never discover their true identities.'

Tim looked up, suddenly intrigued. He said, 'Where do they come from?'

'We don't know,' said Inspector Benedict. 'We never know who they are or where they came from. They have no identification. Usually, they've been floating in the sea for a few weeks or months.' He sighed, then gestured at the landscape surrounding them – the palm trees, the white sand, the clear blue sea. 'Look, this is a beautiful place. We have beautiful beaches here. And beautiful hotels. Everything here is beautiful. But over there...' He pointed across the ocean to the wide, empty horizon. 'Go a thousand miles in that direction and you'll hit Africa. People in Africa are desperate. They have no food. They have no work. Even worse, they know that

35

nothing will change. So they are willing to take crazy risks. They throw themselves into the sea on a piece of wood or an empty barrel. Perhaps some of them manage to find what they're looking for, but most are drowned. Every few months, one of them gets washed up here.'

A junior officer hurried across the beach and muttered a few words in Inspector Benedict's ear.

Inspector Benedict nodded. He closed his notebook and shook hands with Tim and Mrs Malt, thanking them for their help. 'I have to go now,' he said, handing over a white card printed with his name and phone number. 'But please get in touch if you remember anything else. Anything at all, however small, however apparently insignificant. It might help our investigation.'

'There was one other thing,' said Tim.

'Oh, yes?'

'He tried to talk to me.'

'Really? What did he say?'

'I don't know.'

'Did he say one word or many?'

'Just one,' said Tim.

'And what did it sound like?'

'A bit like "collapse".'

'"Collapse",' repeated Inspector Benedict. 'That's interesting.'

'But it might not have been "collapse". It might have been "crystal". Or maybe "cluster". I couldn't really tell.'

'You couldn't understand him?'

'No, not really.'

'He was probably speaking his own language,' said

Inspector Benedict. 'There is no reason that he would have been able to speak English. It might have sounded like "collapse" to you. But perhaps he was saying his own name. Or the name of his village. Or the name of his wife.'

'There's one other thing,' said Tim. 'He said something else too.'

Before Tim could explain what else the drowned man had said, the junior officer muttered to Inspector Benedict, who nodded. He turned to Tim and Mrs Malt. 'Please excuse me,' he said. 'I have to go now. We'll continue this conversation later. Thank you again for all your help.' He turned and hurried across the sand, followed by his junior officer.

Down by the sea, the doctors had placed the body on a stretcher and covered it with a blanket. The policemen cleared a path through the crowd so the stretcher could be carried to an ambulance.

Tim watched two policemen carrying the stretcher along the beach. Two more policemen walked ahead of the stretcher and Inspector Benedict walked behind.

Watching the policemen, Tim thought about the other detail that he hadn't described to the inspector. Perhaps it wasn't important. Perhaps it was.

The drowned man hadn't just said 'collapse' or 'crystal' or 'cluster'. He had said something else too. Something which couldn't have been his own name or the name of his village or the name of his wife. Speaking in English, he had said, 'Help them.'

What had he meant? Help who?

Chapter 11

Tim stared at his plate.

In the centre of the white plate, there was a small lump of grey stuff, sprinkled with pepper. Four triangles of toast lay on the left-hand side of the plate and a dollop of chutney squatted on the right-hand side. Tim knew he should spread the grey stuff on the toast and eat it, but he wasn't sure that he wanted to. He didn't like eating things that he couldn't identify.

Tim looked around the table. The others had been served with exactly the same dish. Max and the Malts had already started eating. Natascha was staring at her plate, frowning.

Mrs Malt saw that Tim wasn't eating. 'This is a great luxury,' she said. 'Aren't you going to try it?'

'I guess,' said Tim.

'You eat it like pâté,' said Mrs Malt. 'Put a little splodge on the toast. Like this.' Mrs Malt cut a slice of the grey stuff, slid it onto a piece of toast and popped it into her mouth. 'Yum,' she said. 'That's delicious. Go on, try it.'

'Okay,' said Tim. He picked up a knife and poked the grey stuff. It was squishy. He did exactly what his mother had done, cutting a slice of the grey stuff and spreading it on the toast. He bit off a corner of the toast and chewed slowly.

The others were watching him, waiting for his reaction.

Mrs Malt said, 'So? What do you think?'

'It's okay,' said Tim. 'What is it?'

'Foie gras,' said Mr Malt. 'Goose liver pâté. One of the greatest delicacies in the world. So you'd better savour every mouthful.'

'Okay,' said Tim. He cut another slice of the grey stuff, spread it on the toast and ate slowly, trying to savour every mouthful.

They were sitting on the terrace at the front of the hotel, overlooking the long sandy beach. The sun had just set. A waiter was walking round the terrace, lighting candles.

Grk was sitting under the table. He kept his eyes open, looking out for dropped food. So far, he had managed to snatch two olives and a cashew nut.

Mr and Mrs Malt were determined that the holiday wasn't going to be spoiled. Something horrible had happened. No one could deny that. But they wouldn't make things any better by moaning about it. Much better, they had decided, to try and enjoy themselves.

Tonight, the Malts had asked Paolo Poulet to prepare a special meal, using the most delicious and luxurious ingredients that the kitchen possessed. Tomorrow, they had hired a boat to take them to a secluded island, their own private paradise, where they could swim in the sea and picnic on the beach, undisturbed by anyone.

Mrs Malt looked around the table. She smiled. Everyone was eating happily. Everyone seemed to be enjoying themselves.

Apart from Natascha.

For some reason, Natascha hadn't even touched her food.

Mrs Malt said, 'Natascha, aren't you hungry?'

'Yes,' said Natascha. 'I'm very hungry.'

'Then why aren't you eating?'

'I don't want this,' said Natascha, pointing at the lump of grey stuff on her plate.

'You should try new foods,' said Mr Malt. 'That's part of the fun of going to different countries.'

Natascha shook her head. 'I don't eat foie gras.'

'Why not?'

'I don't approve of eating a creature which has suffered unnecessarily for my pleasure.'

Natascha was only twelve years old, but she had already formed some strong opinions about life.

'Someone's already killed this,' said Tim, pointing at his plate. 'So we might as well eat it.'

Natascha said, 'Do you know how they make foie gras?'

Tim shook his head. Two minutes ago, he didn't even know that foie gras existed. How could he possibly know how they made it? He said, 'I don't even know what "foie gras" means.'

"Foie gras' is French,' said Natascha. 'It means "fatty liver". They get a goose. They stuff a metal tube down its neck. And they force food down the pipe. They pour masses and masses of corn down the tube. It goes straight down the goose's neck and into its stomach. The goose can't process all that food properly. So its liver swells up to ten times its normal size. The geese become so fat they can't walk. They can't even breathe properly. They just

40

sit there like fat lumps, waiting to be slaughtered.'

'That sounds horrible,' said Tim. He pushed his plate away. 'I'm not eating this.'

Although Mr and Mrs Malt didn't say anything, both of them had stopped eating too. After Natascha's description of force-feeding geese, neither of them felt particularly hungry. They pushed away their plates and sat back in their chairs with their arms folded.

Only Max refused to be dissuaded. He finished every last scrap of his foie gras, even wiping his plate with a piece of toast. 'Mmmm,' he said, licking his lips. 'That was delicious.'

'You're gross,' said Natascha.

Max shrugged his shoulders. 'I like eating meat. I don't see anything wrong with that.'

'Eating meat is gross,' said Natascha. 'And people who eat meat are gross too.'

Max shrugged his shoulders. 'If that's what you think, why don't you become a vegetarian?'

'I will,' said Natascha.

'Good,' said Max.

'Fine,' said Natascha.

They both sat back in their chairs with their arms folded.

Tim looked at each of them in turn. He could never quite decide whether he liked being an only child.

Having a sibling often seemed like fun. There was always someone to talk to. You got more presents at Christmas. You could share friends and clothes and books.

On the other hand, having a sibling seemed a bit like being married. Brothers and sisters, just like husbands and wives, seemed to spend their whole lives disagreeing with one another.

I'm better off alone, thought Tim. I don't want a brother. I don't want a sister. And I definitely never want to get married. I'd rather spend my life alone.

No, he thought. Not quite alone.

He glanced under the table. Grk was lying on the floor, licking his paws.

Just me and Grk, thought Tim. Just the two of us. That's how I want to live my life.

Chapter 12

Every few weeks, Doctor Theodore White got a call from the police. 'There's another one,' they would say. 'It's waiting for you.'

Doctor White would finish whatever he was doing, put a sign in the window of his surgery promising that he would be back in an hour, and drive to the police headquarters. He would show his security pass to get through the front gate. Inside the building, he would put on a white coat and grab a pair of plastic gloves. Accompanied by a policeman, he would go down to the mortuary and inspect whoever had died. When he had finished his inspection, Doctor White wrote a brief report and issued a death certificate, giving the date and the probable cause of death.

Most of the deaths were quite ordinary. Life in the Seychelles was calm and easy. The most common cause of death was old age.

Sometimes, tourists would get themselves killed in more interesting ways, driving off cliffs or falling from boats. You'd be surprised how many people ignored the most basic warnings. Everyone knew, for instance, that you shouldn't lie down in the shade of a coconut tree, because a coconut might fall on your head. Nevertheless, every few years, some foolish tourist decided to have an afternoon nap under a coconut tree and his skull would be smashed into a hundred pieces.

And then there were the ones who were washed ashore.

It happened once or twice a year. A body would be found on one of the beaches. He or she would usually be naked. His or her clothes would have been eaten by the sea and its inhabitants.

In the mortuary, Doctor White prepared to inspect the body, although he already knew that his inspection would be futile. He could have written his report without even looking at the body.

Name: Monsieur X.

Address: unknown.

Nationality: unknown.

Date of birth: unknown.

Date of death: unknown.

Cause of death: drowning.

There are six billion people on the planet. If one of them is swept ashore on your island, how are you supposed to discover their name or the country where they were born?

Doctor White knew the answer to that. You can't. If a man has been floating in the sea for a few months, he has been washed clean. His identity has disappeared. You will never know who he is. In the official records, he would simply be called 'Monsieur X'. That was the name that would be carved on his gravestone.

But Doctor White had a job to do. Even if the procedure was futile, he would still do it. He owed that much to the man who had once inhabited this body. He pulled on his rubber gloves and started his inspection of Monsieur X.

Chapter 13

Max, Natascha, Tim and Grk waited in the lobby, staring at the two big maps pinned to the wall.

It was nine o'clock in the morning. The boat was booked for half past. They were just waiting for Mr and Mrs Malt, then they would go down to the jetty, where the boat would be waiting to take them to a nearby island. They would find a secluded beach and spend a day in perfect solitude. They could have lunch on the sand, swim in the sea and snorkel around the reefs. 'It will be your own private paradise,' Paolo Poulet had promised when he arranged the trip for them.

Looking at the first map, the one showing the island where they were staying, Tim pointed out the place where he had found the drowned man. Max and Natascha tried to decide where they had been taken by the diving instructor. He had sailed round the coast for about half an hour, then anchored opposite a small beach surrounded by black rocks.

They moved to the second map, the one which showed all the islands in the Seychelles, and discussed where they might go today in the boat. They tried to decide how fast the boat would be able to travel and which islands they could reach in a day trip.

Most of the islands had French names, because the Seychelles had been ruled by France for a hundred and fifty years.

Tim whispered some of the names to himself, enjoying their sounds. Silhouette Island. Alphonse Island. Bijoutier Island. Bird Island. Poivre Island. Curieuse Island. Cerf Island. Desroches Island. Marie-Louise Island. Calypso Island. Malabar Island. Les Mamelles Island.

Tim stopped reading. He had the strange sense that one of those names meant something to him. He didn't know why. Or which. But one of them, for some reason, had some special meaning for him.

Have you ever had the sense that your brain is trying to tell you something, but you're not sure what?

Or have you ever been sure that you were supposed to have remembered something, but you can't remember what you might have forgotten?

That's exactly how Tim felt. There was a message waiting for him, deep down in his brain, but he didn't know what it said. And he didn't know how to find out.

He let his eyes wander round the map again, reading more of the names of the islands. Perhaps one of them would spark a particular memory or make him think of something. He recited the names under his breath: Silhouette, Frégate, Cousine, Alphonse, Bijoutier, Poivre, Aldabra, Providence, Curieuse, Desroches, Marie-Louise, Calypso, Bird, Beacon, Malabar, Round, Les Mamelles.

He bit his fingernail. It was so frustrating. He knew that he knew something, but he didn't know what he knew.

He read the names on the map for the third time, letting his eyes wander slowly around the map, reading names at random, whispering them to himself.

This time, one of the names leaped out at him.

Calypso.

Calypso Island.

'That's it,' said Tim. He clapped his hands together. His memory had worked! His brain had done it! He turned to the others with a big grin on his face. 'That's exactly it!'

The others stared at him.

Natascha said, 'That's exactly what?'

Tim said, 'That's what the man was trying to say.'

Max said, 'What are you talking about? Which man?'

'The dead man,' said Tim. 'The man who drowned. The man I found. That's what he said to me. Calypso. The last words he said – that's what they were. Not crystal. Not cluster. Not collapse. Calypso! He wasn't talking some strange language that I couldn't understand. He wasn't saying the name of his wife or his village or anything like that. He was saying Calypso.'

Max said, 'Are you sure?'

Tim nodded. 'I'm absolutely certain. He said "Help them". And then he said "Calypso".'

'What did he mean? What's Calypso?'

'This is Calypso,' said Tim. He placed his finger on the map. 'Right here.'

Max and Natascha leaned forward to see what he was pointing at. Tim's finger was resting on the map beside a small roundish island marked as Calypso. According to the map, the island had no roads, houses or hotels. There wasn't a harbour or a helipad. Calypso Island was just a white blob in the middle of the ocean.

At that moment, Mrs Malt strode into the lobby. 'There you are,' she said in a loud voice. 'We've been searching for you everywhere!'

Her husband hurried after her, carrying two big bags packed with towels and books. 'Come on, come on,' said Mr Malt. 'No time to hang around! The boat will be waiting for us.'

'We can't go yet,' said Tim.

His parents stared at him.

Mr Malt said, 'Can't go? Why not?'

'Because I have to talk to the police.'

Chapter 14

Inspector Benedict was a busy man. Today, he seemed to be even busier than usual. The phones never stopped ringing. His computer never stopped pinging, announcing the arrival of email after email. Papers spurted out of the fax machine.

Nevertheless, Inspector Benedict agreed to see Timothy Malt for five minutes. After all, Timothy Malt wasn't just an ordinary tourist. Timothy Malt was the boy who had discovered the body on the beach.

Tim and Mr Malt sat with Inspector Benedict in his office. On the walls, there were several framed certificates, proving that Inspector Benedict had passed his police exams with top marks. There were some framed photos too, showing Inspector Benedict with several of the celebrities who had visited the Seychelles. Staring at the photos, Tim recognised a pop star, a footballer and a Hollywood actor.

Inspector Benedict explained what the police had discovered about the drowned man's identity. It didn't take long. They had managed to discover just about nothing.

'We have given him a name,' said the Inspector. 'He is now called "Monsieur X". But he remains mysterious to us. Entirely mysterious. There is one particularly strange fact in this case. As you know, once or twice a year, a body is washed up on our shores. They have usually spent several weeks in the sea. Sometimes several months. Their bodies are decayed. But this man isn't like that. He can't have spent more than a day or two in the sea.'

Tim said, 'So what does that mean? Where did he come from?'

'Perhaps he was dumped from a ship,' said Inspector Benedict. 'Over the past few years, there have been rumours. People say that slave ships run across the Indian Ocean, carrying labourers from Africa and India to the Middle East. Perhaps Monsieur X was sailing on one of those ships. Perhaps he was thrown overboard.'

'Or perhaps he was on holiday,' said Tim. 'Perhaps he went swimming in the sea and drowned.'

'Perhaps,' said Inspector Benedict with a smile, amused by the boy's enthusiasm, his eagerness to help solve this crime. 'My men are checking every hotel in the islands. But no concierge has reported a missing guest. I have a feeling that the last days of Monsieur X will remain a mystery.'

'I might be able to help,' said Tim.

'Oh, yes?' said Inspector Benedict. 'And how?'

Tim explained that he now knew what Monsieur X had been trying to say before he died. The drowned man's final words had been 'Help them' and 'Calypso'. Tim was convinced that there must be some connection between Monsieur X and Calypso Island.

Inspector Benedict shook his head. 'I think you must have misunderstood him.'

'I didn't misunderstand anything,' said Tim. 'I know exactly what he said.'

'But it's simply not possible. This man, this Monsieur X, could not have had anything to do with Calypso Island.'

50

'Why not?'

'Because Calypso Island is owned by Edward Goliath,' said Inspector Benedict. 'And Edward Goliath is a very respectable man. You have heard of him?'

Tim shook his head, but Mr Malt nodded. 'He's one of the richest men in the world,' said Mr Malt.

'Exactly,' said Inspector Benedict. 'Edward Goliath is very rich and very powerful. He has important friends and great influence all around the world. It is simply inconceivable that he would have any contact with a person like Monsieur X.'

Tim said, 'Then why did Monsieur X say "Calypso"? Why did he say "Help them" and "Calypso"?'

'Perhaps he didn't,' said Inspector Benedict. 'Perhaps he said something quite different and you simply mis-understood him.'

'I know what he said,' said Tim. 'He said "Calypso" and "Help them". Those were his final words before he died.'

Inspector Benedict nodded. 'Very well. I shall send one of my men to Calypso Island. If possible, I shall go there myself.' He stood up. 'Now, thank you for your help. I am very grateful. But I am also very busy.' He smiled. 'And aren't you supposed to be on holiday?'

'We certainly are,' said Mr Malt.

'Then you shouldn't be sitting inside my office on such a beautiful day. You should be outside, enjoying yourselves.'

Tim said, 'But . . .'

'No buts,' said Inspector Benedict. 'It's an official order from the police. You must go and enjoy yourself.'

51

Chapter 15

Two hours later than the agreed time, the Malts and the Raffifis boarded a small blue motorboat, followed by Grk. Once again, their boatman was Bish. He stood at the wheel with his blue cap pulled down low over his face, shading his eyes from the sun. As he waited for his passengers to settle, he puffed on his cigar and watched them with a steady smile.

When everyone was sitting comfortably, Bish revved the engine. The boat chugged away from the jetty, leaving a trail of white foam and black diesel fumes.

The sea was calm. The sun was hot. Behind them, Mahé slowly faded into the distance and disappeared in a hazy blur.

The boat was quiet and peaceful. While Bish stood at the wheel, staring at the waves, Mr and Mrs Malt sat in the cabin, reading their books.

Natascha hunched over her notebook, scribbling quickly with a black biro, writing notes on the events of the past few days.

Max sat opposite his sister, reading *The Complete Guide to Scuba Diving*. He was determined to pass his test and get a certificate so he could go diving anywhere in the world.

Bish had a pair of binoculars stowed in a locker. He handed them to Tim and showed him how to focus the lenses. Tim lay on the deck beside Grk, staring upwards, watching the huge black birds soar through the clear blue sky. According to Bish, they were called frigate birds.

They had been sailing for about an hour when Bish took the binoculars from Tim and peered through the lenses at the ocean. He had seen something more exciting than a frigate bird. He said, 'Who wants to see a whale?'

'Me,' said Natascha, jumping to her feet. Her journal could wait. A whale was much more exciting.

'Me too,' said Max, dropping his book.

'And me,' said Tim, hurrying to join the others.

Grk didn't say anything, but he sprinted in circles around the cabin, barking loudly. He knew something exciting was happening, although he didn't know what, and he didn't want to be left out.

As the three children crowded round Bish, he said, 'You'll have to take turns. I've only got one pair of these. Here, you first.' He handed the binoculars to Natascha.

She placed the strap around her neck, lifted the binoculars to her eyes and stared at the sea.

Bish said, 'Do you see them?'

'No,' said Natascha.

'Up a bit,' said Bish.

'I can't see anything,' said Natascha.

'Over to the left.'

Natascha said, 'All I can see is...' And then she gasped. 'Oh, that's so beautiful.'

Bish grinned and puffed on his cigar. Surrounded by clouds of grey smoke, he went back to the wheel.

While Bish steered the boat, the three children took turns with the binoculars, watching the whales. They counted five altogether. The huge black shapes eased through the waves, leaving long trails of bubbling foam on the surface of the water.

When they reached the island, Bish anchored the boat in a sheltered cove. There was no sign of humanity – no people, no houses, no boats, no roads, nothing. 'We'll stay here,' said Bish. 'This is a good place.'

Max said, 'Can we swim here?'

'Yes, yes,' said Bish. 'This is a perfect place for swimming.'

Max strapped a mask to his face and flippers to his feet, then popped a snorkel in his mouth and slid off the side of the boat into the water.

Mr Malt lay on a towel, reading a thick novel. Mrs Malt slapped sunscreen over her body, then stretched full-length in the sun and fell asleep. Bish pulled his hat over his eyes and dozed in the shade. Natascha scribbled quickly in her diary, keeping an account of everything that had happened. Grk stretched full-length in the sun and panted. As for Tim – well, while the others were relaxing or reading or writing, Tim was lost in thought.

He thought through the events of the past few days. He thought about Monsieur X. He wondered what could have happened on Calypso Island. He remembered how he had felt, kneeling on the wet sand, staring into the eyes of a man who knew that he was going to die.

'Help them.'

He could almost hear Monsieur X's voice.

'Help them.'

Help who? thought Tim. Who needs help? And where

are they? On Calypso Island? What are they doing there? Did Monsieur X leave them behind? And if so, why? And how? And what is the connection to Edward Goliath? And ... And ... And ... More and more questions crowded into his mind, but he couldn't even begin to find an answer to any of them.

Chapter 16

The blue boat returned to the jetty just before dusk. The Malts and the Raffifis thanked Bish for a great day out and walked back along the beach to the hotel.

At the reception desk, the clerk waved to them. 'Mr Malt? Sir? There is a message for you. From the police.'

The message had been left by Inspector Benedict. He had visited Calypso Island, the message said, and found no trace of Monsieur X. The owner and inhabitants of Calypso Island didn't recognise Monsieur X's name or photograph. They had never seen him. They had nothing suspicious to report. Inspector Benedict thanked the Malts for their help and hoped the rest of their holiday would be peaceful and relaxing.

'Well, there you go,' said Mrs Malt. 'You must have misheard him. He must have said something else.'

'I know exactly what he said,' insisted Tim. 'He said "Calypso".'

'You weren't so sure before,' said Mrs Malt.

'I am now.'

Mr Malt said, 'Don't you remember what Inspector Benedict said?'

'No.'

'I do,' said Mr Malt. 'He ordered you to go and enjoy yourself.'

'But, Dad, how can I enjoy myself when—'

'It was a direct order,' interrupted Mr Malt. 'I really don't think you ought to disobey a direct order from such an important man.'

'He might be wrong.'

'Yes, he might be wrong,' said Mr Malt. 'And he might be right. But it doesn't really matter. It's not our business any more. Our business is having a nice holiday. So let's forget everything that's happened and concentrate on enjoying ourselves. All right?'

'Fine,' said Tim.

Mr Malt said, 'You promise to have fun?'

'I promise,' said Tim.

That evening, Tim tried to have fun.

He tried to smile. He tried to laugh. He tried to enjoy eating supper. He tried to enjoy playing Scrabble. He even tried to enjoy being beaten by Natascha. She got two Scrabbles – TURTLES and RELIEVED – and ended the game with a hundred and eighty-seven points more than anyone else.

Natascha looked at Tim. 'Another game?'

'Sure,' said Tim. 'And this time, I'll win.'

'In your dreams,' said Natascha and scooped up the letters, shovelling them back into the bag.

Later that night, Tim lay in bed, unable to sleep. He had been beaten twice more at Scrabble by Natascha, but that wasn't what kept him awake. There was a much simpler reason why he couldn't sleep. He kept seeing the same vision over and over again.

He saw a man lying on a beach, his arms shaking, his lips

quivering. The man opened his mouth, straining desperately, trying to summon the strength to speak.

But before the man could make a sound, the strength went out of his body. His head dropped back onto the sand. His fingers relaxed. His arms flopped. His eyes rolled in their sockets. He lay still.

There was another person on the beach, squatting in the wet sand, leaning over the man, wanting to help, not knowing what to do.

I could have saved him, thought Tim.

But I failed.

And now I've failed him again. The police don't believe me. They went to the island, but they didn't find anything. So they think I got it wrong. They think I misheard or misunderstood.

But I didn't, thought Tim. I know exactly what he said.

'Calypso,' the drowned man had whispered. 'Help them.' And then he had repeated the name of the island again. 'Calypso.'

Tim sat up in bed. He suddenly realised what he had to do. He would have to visit Calypso Island himself.

It was his responsibility to fulfil Monsieur X's final request.

'Help them.'

He remembered the desperation in Monsieur X's voice. He remembered the expression in Monsieur X's eyes. And, worst of all, he remembered his own feelings of helplessness and incompetence.

'Help them.'

Tim felt sick with guilt. He had failed to save a man's

life. Well, there was only one thing for him to do. He had to fulfil the dying man's last request. He had to make a trip to Calypso Island. He had to 'help them' – whoever they might be.

Chapter 17

In the morning, Tim felt much better. He had a shower and got dressed, then went downstairs for breakfast. On his way to the restaurant, he paused in the lobby and looked at the map of all the islands in the Seychelles. He stared at Mahé and Calypso, the island where he was now and the island where he wanted to go. Between them, there was a large expanse of blue.

Tim walked to the reception desk. The clerk was chatting to another guest. She turned to Tim and said, 'Good morning, sir. Can I help?'

Tim said, 'Do you know Calypso Island?'

'I know where it is,' said the clerk.

'How do I get there?'

The clerk shook her head. 'I'm afraid that wouldn't be possible. Calypso is closed to tourists. It's a private island.'

'Couldn't I just visit?'

'No, sir. You're not allowed to set foot on a private island. It would be like walking into someone else's house. You can't do that unless they invite you inside. But we have many other beautiful islands in the Seychelles which you're more than welcome to visit. Here, let me give you a map.' She reached under the counter and pulled out a colourful brochure. 'This has information about all the islands that are open to the public and how you can reach them.'

'Thanks,' said Tim, taking the brochure. 'Will you tell

me one thing? I know I'm not allowed to visit Calypso Island. But if I did, how long would it take to get there?'

The clerk reached under the counter, pulled out another brochure and spread it flat. She traced a line with her finger between Mahé and Calypso. 'That would take about half an hour in a helicopter,' said the clerk. 'Or three hours in a boat. A little more, maybe, or a little less, depending on the weather.'

'Thanks,' said Tim. 'Thanks a lot.'

He stood in the middle of the lobby for a couple of minutes, looking at the brochure and thinking through his plan. He knew what to do. Now, he just had to do it.

He tucked the brochure in his pocket, walked through the lobby and went to find the others in the restaurant. They were already eating breakfast.

Mr Malt put down his coffee cup and said, 'Good morning, Tim. How are you?'

'Dot doo bad,' said Tim in a completely different voice to the clear tones that he had used when talking to the clerk.

Mr Malt blinked and peered at his son. 'What did you say?'

'Dot doo bad,' repeated Tim.

'Did you sleep well?'

'Des, tanks,' said Tim. 'Bery bell.'

Mrs Malt looked at her son with a worried expression. She said, 'What's wrong with your voice?'

'By dose is blocked,' said Tim.

'Oh dear.' Mrs Malt reached to her son and placed her hand on his forehead. It felt a bit warm. She said, 'Your cold isn't any better?'

61

Tim shook his head. 'Do,' he said. 'Buch burse.'

Mr Malt blinked. 'Buch burse?'

'Des,' said Tim. 'Buch burse.'

Mr Malt thought for a moment. Then he smiled. 'Oh, you mean "much worse". Your cold is much worse.'

'Des,' said Tim. 'By cold is buch burse.'

Mr and Mrs Malt glanced at one another. They had been planning to take Tim on a special diving expedition which would make him forget all about Monsieur X. But if Tim still had a cold, he couldn't go diving. So what were they going to do?

Mrs Malt said, 'Terence, let's go and have a little walk on the terrace.'

Mr Malt looked down at his bowl. He had just started eating a bowl of delicious muesli smothered with fresh mango, melon, pineapple and bananas. He said, 'Could we go in two minutes? I'd quite like to finish my breakfast.'

'I think we should go now,' said Mrs Malt, using that tone of voice which could not be disobeyed.

'Yes, dear,' said Mr Malt, getting to his feet. He cast one last lingering look at his breakfast, then followed his wife through the restaurant.

Mr and Mrs Malt paced up and down the terrace together, talking in whispers. After five minutes, they returned to the table with smiles on their faces. They both sat down. Mr Malt started spooning muesli into his mouth. Mrs Malt said, 'We're going to go for another boat trip. And this time, we'll go to a different island. Doesn't that sound fun?'

Mr and Mrs Malt had decided to cancel the diving.

Instead, they would go in a boat together and have a picnic lunch on a different island. That way, Tim wouldn't feel left out. He wouldn't have to sit alone while the others went diving.

Max and Natascha were disappointed. They would have preferred to dive again. But they concealed their disappointment and pretended that nothing could possibly be more fun than a day in a boat.

Tim was even more disappointed. His cunning plan had failed. He wouldn't spend the day alone. He wouldn't have a chance to sneak aboard a boat or a helicopter. He couldn't grab a ride to Calypso Island. And, even worse, he would have to spend the whole day talking in a silly voice, pretending his nose was still blocked.

Then he had an idea.

Tim said, 'By don't bey bo bibing?'

The others stared at him.

Mr Malt said, 'What?'

Mrs Malt said, 'Did you just say "By don't bey bo bibing?"'

'Bat's bright,' said Tim.

'Well, what on earth did you mean by that?'

'Bax and Ashasha,' said Tim. 'Bey can bo bibing. By don't bind.' Everyone was staring at him with expressions of complete puzzlement, but he didn't want to stop speaking in the voice of a man with a very blocked nose. He wanted everyone to think he was ill. 'By should bey have to suffer dust because bime bill? Bat's not fair. Bet bem bo bibing.'

Mr Malt scratched his head. 'Bet bem bo bibing?'

'Des,' said Tim. 'Bet bem bo bibing.'

Chapter 18

It took a little time for Mr Malt to realise that when Tim said, 'Bet bem bo bibing', he was actually saying, 'Let them go diving.' It took even longer for Mr and Mrs Malt to discuss whether two children should do one activity while the third did another. But once that was decided, everything else could be arranged very quickly.

Paolo Poulet promised to find another boat for the Malts. He asked his chef to prepare another picnic lunch. He himself made a few suggestions for interesting islands to visit. Before making a phone call to book a boat, he had just one final question. 'And with the boat, do you wish for a driver?'

'No, no,' said Mr Malt. 'We don't need to hire a driver. We'll go alone.'

'You were not happy with Bish?'

'Bish was great,' said Mr Malt. 'He was perfect. But we'd rather go alone today.'

Paolo Poulet frowned. 'It is more safe to have a driver. He knows how to handle a boat. He knows the islands. With a driver, nothing will go wrong. If you go alone, there is the possibility of accidents.'

Mr Malt smiled. 'Nothing will go wrong. I spent yesterday watching Bish. He showed me what to do. Anyway, I could do all that even without Bish's help. I know exactly how to handle a boat.'

'Do you?' said Tim. He didn't know his dad could

handle boats. 'How?'

Mr Malt said, 'When I was a boy, we used to stay in Devon for a fortnight every summer. I spent all day messing about in boats. I had an Enterprise.'

Natascha said, 'What's an Enterprise?'

'A lovely little dinghy. She was fourteen foot long with a blue sail. Gosh, she was so beautiful.' Mr Malt suddenly looked quite wistful. 'Her name was *Over Easy*. And she did turn over easily. But when she stayed upright, she went so fast through the water, you thought you were going to take off.'

Mrs Malt said, 'Terence, are you sure about this?'

'Quite sure,' said Mr Malt.

'Really, Terence? Are you absolutely sure you know what you're doing?'

'You have my word,' said Mr Malt. 'You'll have the best day of your life.'

Mrs Malt wasn't convinced. The idea of taking off didn't really appeal to her. The idea of turning over, however easily, appealed even less. 'Maybe we should take a driver,' she said. 'Just in case something goes wrong.'

'Nothing will go wrong,' said Mr Malt. 'As I said, I spent the whole of my childhood messing around on boats. I know exactly what I'm doing.' He turned to Paolo Poulet. 'We'll hire a boat and take a picnic lunch, but we don't want a driver.'

'As you wish,' said Paolo Poulet. 'I will arrange for the boat to be waiting for you in one hour.'

Chapter 19

An hour later, Bish drove a red motorboat to the jetty and tied it up beside the blue boat. Percy was already inside the blue boat, tinkering with the engine.

As always, a cigar drooped from Bish's lips and his wrinkled face was shaded by an old blue cap. He eased the boat to a standstill, strode down the deck, grabbed a rope and hopped ashore. For a man who couldn't have been less than sixty, and might have been seventy, he moved with amazing speed and grace. He looped the rope around a cleat on the jetty, then turned to the five people waiting there. 'All yours, my friends,' said Bish. He gestured at the Malts. 'For you, one boat and no driver.' He turned and gestured at the Raffifis. 'And for you, one boat and two drivers.' Then Bish gestured at himself. 'And for me? For me, just one cigar.' He grinned and puffed on his cigar. Within moments, his face was shrouded in clouds of grey smoke.

Max and Natascha clambered aboard the blue boat with Bish and Percy. Mr Malt, Mrs Malt, Tim and Grk boarded the red boat.

Mrs Malt stowed the bags in the lockers. Grk stood on the prow, sniffing the sea breeze, then turned to stare across the jetty at Max and Natascha. His tail drooped. He didn't understand what was happening. Why were the Malts and the Raffifis boarding different boats? Were they going to sail in different directions? Was this the last time that they would ever see one another?

In the locker, Mrs Malt found the life jackets. She insisted that Tim wore one.

'Bi don't banna bear a dife wacket,' said Tim. 'Bi bont ball in.'

'Your father's driving this boat,' replied Mrs Malt. 'So anything might happen. Come on, put it on.' Ignoring Tim's protests, she lifted the life jacket over Tim's head, then tied the straps around his middle.

When they were all wearing their life jackets, Mr Malt stood at the wheel and saluted to Bish. 'Untie us, please.'

'Yes, boss,' said Bish, hurrying along the jetty. He untied the rope from the cleat and threw it aboard the boat.

Mr Malt revved the throttle. He turned the wheel. The boat chugged away from the jetty and headed towards the open sea.

Bish stood on the shore with a smile on his face, puffing his cigar and waving. From the deck of the blue boat, Max and Natascha waved too.

Tim and his parents waved back. Then Mr Malt turned to face forwards and pulled the throttle. The engine roared. The boat accelerated through the water, leaving a path of white foam and frothing bubbles.

The red boat and the blue boat went in different directions. As the red boat headed towards the open sea, the blue boat chugged away from the jetty and skirted the island.

Percy stood at the wheel of the blue boat. Max and Natascha sat in the stern with Bish. Max quizzed Bish about diving. He wanted to know the answers to all kinds of questions. What was the biggest shark that Bish had ever seen? Does swordfish taste good? When do turtles lay their eggs? How do you recognise a poisonous jellyfish? What's the difference between a dolphin and a porpoise?

Natascha made notes on their conversation, writing down a few interesting facts which she thought might be useful. She had decided to write a travel article about the Seychelles. When she got back to London, she would send the article to several newspapers and see if she could get it published.

In the red boat, Mr Malt stood at the wheel, grinning like a happy schoolboy. He was having such fun! The splashing waves, the smell of salt, the sound of the engine, the feeling of the boat beneath him – he hadn't enjoyed anything so much in years.

He held the wheel with one hand and a chart with the other, plotting their progress towards a deserted island where they would stop for lunch. Every now and then, he glanced at the compass, checking that the boat was keeping to the right course. Occasionally, he glanced at the horizon, checked for other boats or looked out for islands. But mostly he remembered being twelve years old and sailing a small dinghy around the creeks and bays near Salcombe, a village in Devon.

He hadn't thought about Salcombe for years. And now he couldn't think of anything else.

He'd never felt so free since those glorious days. Every morning, he had taken out the boat with nothing for company except a bottle of lemonade and a packet of sandwiches. Every day, he had sailed from one end of the estuary to the other, exploring islands and coves, stopping to eat his lunch on a deserted beach.

When Mr Malt was sixteen, his parents stopped going to Salcombe and started going to France on their holidays instead. Two years later, Mr Malt went to university and considered himself too old to go on holidays with his parents. Since then, he had never been in a dinghy or even sailed a boat. He had never been back to Devon. And he had never felt so free.

Mr Malt stared at the horizon with a big grin on his face. When he got back to England, he had decided, he was going to make a few changes in his life. He was going to take a sailing course. He was going to think about buying a boat. And maybe he was going to do something even more radical too. Next year, he was going to suggest to his wife that they went somewhere different for their holidays. Not Kenya. Not Iceland. Not the Seychelles. Rather than trying to find paradise at the other end of a ten-hour flight, they should get on a train and go to Devon.

The blue boat reached a small cove. The rocky shore was surrounded by tall palm trees. Max and Natascha leaned over the side of the boat and peered down through the clear water. They could see all kinds of interesting patterns and colours on the bottom of the ocean.

Bish looked at the two children. 'You both want to dive?'

'Yes, please,' said Natascha.

'Definitely,' said Max.

'Then let's get ready.' Bish pulled the diving equipment from the locker, spreading masks, weights and bottles along the bottom of the boat. 'I hope you can remember everything I taught you last time.'

Max and Natascha both nodded confidently.

'In that case, we'll have a little test,' said Bish. 'So, Max, what is a BCD?'

Max said, 'A buoyancy control device.'

'Very good.' Bish turned to Natascha. 'Now, your turn. What is nitrogen narcosis?'

Natascha opened her notebook and flicked through the pages.

'No, no,' said Bish. 'No looking in the book. Doesn't matter what you wrote down. What you remember – that's what matters. Come on, you can remember. What's nitrogen narcosis?'

Natascha thought for a minute, then shook her head. 'I've forgotten.'

Bish turned to Max. 'Do you know?'

'Nitrogen narcosis is like being drunk,' said Max. 'It's a condition caused by being underwater. You lose your judgement and do stupid things which could easily lead to drowning. It's one more reason to be very careful when you dive.'

'Very good,' said Bish. 'Now, who can remember how to put a mask on?' He handed a diving mask to each of the children. Without any hesitation, Max strapped the mask onto his face. Natascha turned her mask over and over in her hands, trying to remember the right way that it should be worn.

*

As the red boat ploughed through the waves, its occupants were quiet. Each of them was lost in their own thoughts.

Mr Malt stood at the wheel, dreaming about his childhood holidays. Mrs Malt sat in the stern, reading a thick paperback with a glossy cover, immersed in the story's twists and turns. Tim and Grk sat together at the front of the boat. When the bow plunged against a big wave, they got covered in a shower of spray, but it was cool and refreshing, and the hot sun soon dried Tim's clothes and Grk's fur.

A dog's thoughts are hidden from humans, so I can't tell you what Grk was thinking about. I can, however, tell you exactly what Tim was thinking about. He was trying to make a plan. He was trying to imagine a way to escape from his parents and reach Calypso Island.

Tim didn't hate his parents. Quite the opposite. He rather liked them. They provided him with the necessities of life – food, clothing, shelter – and didn't ask too much in return. However, he didn't trust them. He couldn't tell them his secrets or his plans. He knew that they wouldn't just disagree with him, they would try to stop him. They would say such things should be left to the proper authorities. They would say the police undoubtedly knew what they were doing. They would say Tim wasn't old enough to be independent and he couldn't possibly discover the secrets of Calypso Island alone.

Perhaps they were right. Perhaps the police did know what they were doing. Perhaps Tim was too young to do such things for himself. But none of that mattered. He had an obligation to Monsieur X. An obligation which he was determined to fulfil. Somehow, he would have to escape his parents and make his own way to Calypso Island.

He stood up, clambered along the side of the boat and hopped down into the cockpit. Grk hurried after him.

Tim stood beside his father. He looked at the wheel, the compass and the chart. He stared at the horizon ahead. Then he said, 'Bad?'

'Hello,' said Mr Malt.

'Bill you beach me how to bive a boat?'

Mr Malt looked at his son. 'Will I what?'

'Bill you beach me how to bive a boat?'

'Will I teach you how to drive a boat?'

'Exactly,' said Tim. 'Bill you beach me how to bive a boat?'

A smile spread slowly across Mr Malt's face. 'Of course I will. Here, come and stand beside me. Put your hands on the wheel.'

Tim stood beside his father and put his hands on the wheel.

Mr Malt lifted his own hands off the wheel. 'There you go,' said Mr Malt. 'Now you're steering. How does that feel?'

'Good,' said Tim.

'Try turning it a bit.'

'Okay,' said Tim. He turned the wheel to the left, then the right, and felt the boat turning through the water, obeying his instructions.

'Perfect,' said Mr Malt. He pointed at one of the dials on the dashboard. 'Do you see that dial? That's your speed.' He pointed at another dial. 'And that's the depth of the water underneath the boat. It doesn't matter now, because we're in the middle of the ocean, but you have to watch that carefully when you come close to land. Otherwise you'll run aground.'

Tim said, 'How do you navigate?'

'You use the chart and the compass,' said Mr Malt. 'Do you want me to show you?'

Tim nodded. 'Yes, please.'

Tim had forgotten to speak in a funny voice, but it didn't really matter. Both he and his father were so fascinated by the mechanics of sailing a boat, neither of them noticed the sudden and miraculous disappearance of Tim's cold.

Mr Malt unfolded the chart. He pointed at an island. 'This is where we started.' He pointed at a blank blue patch in the middle of the ocean. 'This is roughly where we are now.' He pointed at another island. 'And this is where we want to go. You have to plot a course from one to the other, then follow the course using the compass.'

'How?' said Tim.

'I'm just about to show you. But first I'll tell you something even more important. What to do in an emergency.'

Mr Malt left Tim holding the wheel, went to the back of the boat and searched through the cupboards. He returned with a small red tube which looked like a firework. 'Do you know what this is?'

Tim shook his head.

'A flare,' said Mr Malt. 'If you get in trouble, you fire this into the air. It's like a firework. It shoots up into the air and explodes in a big cloud of red smoke. With any luck, someone will see it and come and rescue you.'

Mr Malt showed Tim how to use the flare, making him practise again and again until he knew exactly what to do. 'One day,' said Mr Malt, 'a flare like this might save your life.' Tim wanted to practise properly and fire a flare into the air, but his father wouldn't let him. Someone might see the smoke, he explained, assume a sailor was in danger and call the coastguard.

When Mr Malt was sure that Tim knew how to use the flare, he explained what to do in other possible emergencies. How to survive a storm. How to avoid being run down by a ferry or a tanker in thick fog. What to do if your boat starts leaking or a big wave turns your boat upside down.

Smiling as he recalled one of the happiest days of his youth, Mr Malt described the day that his dinghy capsized in the middle of the ocean, half a mile from the coast of Devon, and how he managed to save his own life.

Tim took careful note of exactly what his father said, trying to remember everything, even the smallest details.

Chapter 20

'There it is,' said Mr Malt. 'That's where we're going.' He pointed straight ahead. 'That's Aubergine Island. Highly recommended by Bish as the perfect place for lunch and snorkelling.'

The three of them stared at a low shape on the horizon.

Mrs Malt said, 'What an odd name.'

'Apparently it looks like an aubergine,' said Mr Malt. He put his hand to his forehead, shading his eyes from the sun, and peered at the island. 'You probably have to be looking at it from the right angle.'

As they came closer, the shape became larger and clearer. Soon, they could see that it was a small, flattish island, covered with a forest of palm trees. Big grey rocks lay scattered along the shore as if they'd been dropped from the sky. Stretches of yellow sand shone in the bright sunlight.

According to Bish, the only creatures who lived on Aubergine Island were birds, beetles and bugs. The occasional turtle crawled onto the sand to lay some eggs, then scurried back into the sea, leaving its babies to fend for themselves when they popped out of their shells. Humans hardly ever visited the island. If you happened to coincide with another party of tourists, you might see a boat moored in a bay or some bodies lying on a beach. But if no one else chose to come to Aubergine Island on the same day as you, the rocks, trees and sand would be entirely yours.

Mr Malt headed for a small bay. He ordered Tim to grab the anchor and unwrap a good length of rope.

As they approached the long sandy beach, Mr Malt slowed the engine to a gentle chug. He sent Tim to the front of the boat, arming him with precise instructions.

The boat eased towards the shore. When they reached shallow water, Mr Malt shouted, 'Now, Tim! Jump!'

Tim stared down at the water. He wasn't sure that he wanted to jump. It looked cold and deep.

'Jump!' shouted Mr Malt. 'Go on! Jump!'

Mrs Malt stared at her husband. 'He shouldn't jump in the water,' she said. 'He's got a terrible cold.'

'He'll be fine,' said Mr Malt. 'A bit of water never hurt anyone.' He shouted down the length of the boat at his son. 'Now, Tim! Jump now!'

Tim took a deep breath and jumped overboard. He landed in the waves with a big splash. The water came up to his waist. It was cold, but not too cold. He waded ashore, carrying the anchor, and walked up the beach until he reached the nearest tree. Remembering his father's instructions, he wrapped the rope three times around the tree, then wedged the anchor into the sand.

Mr and Mrs Malt slid off the boat and waded through the water to the beach. Mr Malt checked what Tim had done with the anchor, then nodded. 'Well done,' he said. 'That's perfect. You're going to be a good sailor, I can tell.'

When they were settled on the beach, Mrs Malt spread a couple of blankets on the hot sand, making sure that she didn't place them directly under the palm trees. Although the shade would have been welcome, she didn't want to be crushed by a falling coconut. She unpacked their lunch from the brown hamper that had been prepared by the chef at the Hotel Sea Shell.

Mr Malt had brought a penknife. Using the corkscrew, he opened the bottle of white wine. He poured some wine into two plastic glasses, then put the bottle back in the icebox to keep cool.

They sat on the blankets and ate the picnic. The chef had made sandwiches with thick slices of ham inside crispy baguettes. There were roast chicken legs and three types of cheese. There were juicy tomatoes and a crisp cucumber. There were oranges, apples and mangoes. Six boiled eggs nestled in a brown paper bag. Buried at the bottom of the hamper, Mrs Malt found twists of silver foil holding salt and pepper.

Mr and Mrs Malt shared the bottle of white wine. Tim drank orange juice. He tipped half a bottle of water onto a plastic plate for Grk to lap up.

Holding a chicken leg in one hand and his wine in the other, Mr Malt said, 'Isn't this fun?'

'Such fun,' said Mrs Malt. 'So relaxing. I couldn't imagine a more perfect holiday.'

'I'll drink to that.' Mr Malt lifted his glass. 'Cheers.'

Mr and Mrs Malt clinked their plastic glasses and drank. Then, they both turned to look at their son. Mrs Malt said, 'How about you, Tim? Are you having a nice day?'

Tim nodded.

Mr Malt said, 'Did you enjoy the boat trip?'

Tim nodded again. He was thinking about something else. He didn't have time to make polite chitchat.

'Good,' said Mr Malt. He turned to his wife. 'I've had

77

a brilliant idea. When we get back to England, we should buy a boat.'

'A boat? What kind of boat?'

'A dinghy,' said Mr Malt. 'We could keep it on the Thames. We could go sailing every weekend.'

Mrs Malt had a fixed smile on her face. She said, 'Who'd like another egg?'

As I'm sure you know, swimming on a full stomach can be dangerous and even deadly. You should always wait at least an hour after eating before venturing into the sea.

After lunch, Mrs Malt lay down on the blankets that she had spread on the sand. Mr Malt lay beside her.

Grk walked three times in a circle and curled up on a comfy patch of sand.

Tim lay down on the sand too, but he didn't let himself doze off. He watched his parents through half-closed eyes.

Mr Malt had drunk three glasses of white wine. Mrs Malt had drunk two. The sun was hot. The air was warm. The only sounds were the waves washing rhythmically against the shore and the leaves rustling gently in the trees.

After about five minutes, Mr Malt started snoring.

Two or three minutes later, a little line of spit dribbled out of Mrs Malt's mouth and wriggled down her chin.

When that happened, Tim knew that they were both asleep. He stood up and padded slowly across the hot sand, taking great care not to make any noise. Grk bounded after him.

Chapter 21

Tim didn't want to leave his parents completely mystified by his disappearance. They might worry that he'd gone swimming too quickly after lunch, got cramp and sunk. Or they might suspect that he'd been eaten by an enormous lizard.

You might think that you wouldn't find many enormous lizards on tropical islands, but you would be wrong. An old friend of mine once spent several weeks on a tropical island. One afternoon, he realised that his wife had gone missing. He walked along the beach and through the jungle, calling her name. Finally, he found one of her sandals under a tree. An enormous lizard was lurking nearby, looking very pleased with itself. He killed the lizard and cut it open. Inside the lizard's stomach, he found not only the second sandal, but most of his wife too. If you ever take a trip to a tropical island, keep your eyes open for enormous lizards. They may not eat all your footwear, but they will eat you.

Tim didn't want his parents to worry that he had drowned in the sea or been eaten by an enormous lizard. So he walked down the beach until he found a long stick.

He walked back again, carrying the long stick, and chose a flat patch of sand, not far from the spot where his parents were sleeping. Using the stick, he scrawled six words in the sand. He wrote the letters as big as possible so no one could possibly fail to notice them. This is what he wrote:

TOOK BOAT
BACK SOON
LOVE TIM

He hoped the letters wouldn't be washed away by the sea or blown aside by the wind before his parents woke up and had a chance to read them.

As Tim stared at the letters, he felt guilty. He didn't like abandoning his parents. But he couldn't think of any alternative. He had to fulfil Monsieur X's last request. He had to go to Calypso Island and *help them* – whoever *they* might be. He was sure that if his parents knew where he was going and what he was doing, they would try to stop him. So he had no choice. He had to sneak away without telling them where he was going.

Tim dropped the stick on the sand and walked along the beach to the anchor. Grk followed him.

When Tim reached the anchor, he looked at Grk. He whispered, 'Do you want to come with me? Or would you rather stay here with Mum and Dad?'

Grk wagged his tail.

Tim wasn't sure what that meant. By wagging his tail, Grk might have been saying, 'Yes, please, I'd like to come with you.' Or, just as easily, he might have been saying, 'Are you completely out of your mind? I'd much rather stay here.'

Tim whispered, 'Which is it? Are you going to come with me? Or would you rather stay here?'

Grk just wagged his tail even faster.

'Fine,' whispered Tim. 'I'll choose for you. You can come with me.'

Tim picked up the anchor and unwound the rope that was wrapped around the tree. Carrying the anchor and the rope, he walked down to the boat. Grk followed him to the edge of the beach. When Tim went into the water, Grk stayed on the sand. Grk didn't like swimming. As far as Grk was concerned, swimming was no different to taking a bath in an enormous tub and Grk hated baths.

Tim waded through the water, coiling the rope as he went, then dropped the anchor and the rope into the boat. He waded back again and picked Grk up. Carrying Grk in his arms, he waded through the shallows to the boat, pushed Grk aboard and scrambled after him.

Tim sat in the driver's seat. Grk perched beside him, peering over the top of the windscreen.

Remembering his father's instructions, Tim started the engine.

A thunderous growl roared across the ocean, echoing round the bay. Tim winced. He couldn't believe that anyone could sleep through such a loud noise. Any minute, he was sure, he would hear his father's stern voice and his mother's angry screams, ordering him to switch off the engine and return to the island with the boat.

He glanced back.

On the beach, his parents were lying exactly as he had left them. They hadn't moved. Perhaps they were just opening their eyes, wondering what on earth that noise was.

Tim knew he had to be quick. He turned the wheel. The boat chugged out of the bay and headed for the open sea.

Chapter 22

For a long time, Tim drove the boat through the vast empty ocean. The world was reduced to a few simple facts: the sun, the sky, the sea. The sun was hot. The sky was cloudless. The sea went on for ever. Tim felt very small.

He passed a few other yachts and motorboats, but none came close. They were just specks on the ocean, a black hull or a white sail, so far away that he couldn't even distinguish the shapes of any people aboard.

He saw some islands. From one, he noticed a trail of smoke rising into the sky. From another, he spotted a speck moving through the air which might have been a bird or a helicopter.

Two terns came to investigate the boat. They circled twice, then flew away.

Once, a dark shape broke the surface, no more than a hundred metres from the boat. It might have been a dolphin or a whale. Tim was tempted to go and have a closer look, but he resisted the temptation. He didn't have time for sightseeing. He just pointed the boat in the direction of Calypso Island and went full speed ahead.

The boat rolled gently from side to side, rising over a wave and dropping down the other side. The wind brushed against Tim's face, fiddling with his hair. Water splashed against the side of the boat, sending a fine spray into the air. Every now and then, Tim got soaked, but the hot sun soon dried him off.

Tim didn't have a watch, so he didn't know how long he had been travelling. Maybe two hours. Maybe three or four.

Grk lay at Tim's feet, carefully keeping his entire body in the shade. He wasn't asleep, but he didn't seem entirely awake either. He panted quickly, his pink tongue dangling between his jaws.

Just like Grk, Tim was hot and thirsty. If he searched the boat, perhaps he could have found a bottle of water, but he didn't dare leave his post. He stood with both hands on the wheel, staring at the horizon, glancing at the compass, guiding the boat, hoping he was heading in the right direction, praying he hadn't forgotten anything that his father had taught him.

On the chart, the route looked so simple. Here was Aubergine Island. There was Calypso Island. A short stretch of blue separated them.

But sailing across the ocean was very different to plotting a course on a chart. On the map, the blue emptiness looked small and straightforward. In the middle of the ocean, the blue emptiness was vast and terrifying. You could be lost for days without seeing another person. You could starve. You could die of thirst. You could vanish and no one would notice.

Tim stood in the cockpit and stared at the sea. Wherever he looked, he could just see sky and water. Nothing else. Nothing but sky and water.

He had become so bored, so tired and so mesmerised by the monotony of the journey that he forgot to look for the island. He stopped searching the horizon. He just drove forwards across the ocean, his hands on the wheel, his eyes glancing at the compass every few seconds to check his course.

And then he saw it.

A low shape. The island. His destination.

It didn't look anything special. As if someone had rubbed the sky into the sea and left a black smudge on the horizon.

For a long time, while the boat chugged closer to the island, nothing changed. Then, minute by minute, the island took shape, and Tim could see an increasing number of its features.

It was a long, low island, covered with palm trees. Waves broke against the rocky shore. Here and there, patches of white sand glistened in the sunlight.

Tim could distinguish a line of trees along the shore and big black rocks studding the beach. He couldn't see houses, boats, helicopters or any other sign of human presence.

He didn't know what he would find on Calypso Island. He didn't know whether to approach the island from one side or the other. He didn't know what he should be looking for. So he just drove the boat forwards and kept watching, hoping that when he saw something important, he would recognise it as being important.

As Tim sped towards the island, he had a sudden, surprising thought.

He knew how to start the boat. He knew how to steer

with the wheel and plot his course with the compass. But he didn't know how to stop the boat.

Earlier that day, when the time had come to moor, Mr Malt had stood in the cockpit and sent Tim to the front of the boat. Tim had waited in the bows with the anchor in his hands, listening for his father's shouted instructions. When his father yelled 'Jump!', he had jumped.

But now he was alone. And he didn't know what to do.

He couldn't go and stand at the front of the boat with the anchor, because that would leave no one standing in the cockpit, grasping the wheel, steering the boat in the right direction.

Unless Grk took the wheel. But Tim didn't have much faith in Grk's ability as a sailor.

What else could he do?

Thinking through his options, Tim realised he didn't even know how to switch off the engine.

In different circumstances, Tim might have got depressed. He might have sat in a corner with his arms folded, feeling sorry for himself. He might even have wiped a couple of tears from the corners of his eyes.

But he didn't have time for any of that stuff now. He was driving at high speed towards the shore of a strange island in a boat that he didn't know how to stop. He could get depressed later. He could even shed a tear or two. Right now, he had to save his skin.

Tim pulled the throttle. Nothing happened. He pushed the throttle. Nothing continued to happen. He twiddled the throttle. Nothing just kept happening.

Tim panicked. He didn't know what to do. He pulled levers and pushed buttons. Lights flashed. Dials spun.

But the engine continued roaring and the boat continued moving and the shore came closer and closer.

Tim had a brilliant idea: he had switched on the engine by twisting the key, so he must be able to switch off the engine by twisting the key.

He twisted the key.

Nothing happened.

He twisted the key again, back and forth, up and down, round and round.

Nothing happened.

Only now, as he approached the island, did Tim realise how fast he had been travelling. The red boat was moving through the water like a rocket.

Several terns lifted into the air and wheeled away, screeching.

Tim could see the shore clearly now. There was a long sandy beach fringed with tall palm trees. Heavy dark rocks dotted the sand. Any minute now, thought Tim, this boat will be wrapped around one of those rocks. And I'll be dead.

He let go of the wheel and dropped to the floor, wedging himself against the cabin, preparing himself for the impact. Then he remembered Grk. He looked up.

Grk was lying in the middle of the floor, panting, completely unaware that in five or ten seconds from now, his world would be turned upside down.

'Come here,' yelled Tim.

Grk lifted his head, stared at Tim and blinked.

'Come on!' shouted Tim.

Grk panted.

'Come here!' shouted Tim. 'Right now!'

Grk blinked and panted.

Tim opened his mouth to shout again, but before he could utter a single word, the boat lurched violently. There was a terrible bang, followed by the loudest screech that Tim had ever heard.

The boat had cut through the shallow water surrounding the island and rammed into the beach. Momentum sent it shooting out of the water onto the sand.

Tim was thrown backwards, then forwards. He tried to grab something for support, but his fingers couldn't get a grip on anything. He spun round the bottom of the boat, thumping every part of his body.

Metal roared. Sand crunched. Water splashed. The boat shook and shuddered and slammed into the trunk of a tall palm tree. The front of the boat buckled and broke. Tim and Grk were tossed forwards by the impact, then thrown backwards.

Tim smacked his head against a cupboard door and slumped to the floor with a terrible groan. His eyes rolled in their sockets and he lost consciousness.

Grk spun across the floor, rolling one way, then the other, and came to a standstill in the bottom of the boat, his four legs spread-eagled in different directions.

Then the coconuts fell on them.

Right at the top of the palm tree, there were three large hairy coconuts, which had been waiting for the perfect moment to drop.

Who knows when that moment might have been. A tug of wind, perhaps, blowing off the sea, might have gently pulled one of the coconuts from its perch. The beak of a parrot, pecking at the surrounding leaves, could have dislodged another. The third might just have decided to drop down to the ground in the middle of a warm, calm afternoon.

But these three coconuts were knocked to the ground by something quite unexpected. A red motorboat rammed into the base of their tree, thumping the trunk with enormous force. All three coconuts immediately plummeted, gathering speed as they fell.

The first coconut smacked onto the front of the boat like a cannonball. There was a loud bang. The coconut snapped in two, spilling its juice.

The second coconut smashed through the windscreen, knocking shards of glass in every direction.

The third coconut slammed into the cockpit, missing Tim by inches, leaving a massive dent in the metal.

Those three bangs would have been loud enough to wake just about anyone, but they didn't wake Tim. He lay on the bottom of the boat, not moving. His mouth was open. His eyes were shut. A trickle of blood ran down his forehead.

Chapter 23

Mr Malt opened his eyes. For a second, he couldn't remember where he was. He could see sand. He could feel hot sun on his skin. He could hear waves gently splishing and sploshing. And then he remembered. Of course, he thought. I'm on holiday. I'm lying on a tropical island. I'm in paradise.

With a big smile on his face, Mr Malt sat up, stretched his arms into the air and looked around. In every direction, he could see nothing except perfection. It was like a postcard or a brochure. White sand. Blue sky. Clear sea. Hot sun. This really was paradise. He'd be happy to stay here forever.

There was just one slight problem. His head ached. Perhaps he was dehydrated. Drinking wine at lunchtime often gave him a headache. Mr Malt grabbed a bottle of water, took a sip, and thought about swimming. He must have been asleep for more than an hour. His lunch would be thoroughly digested by now. He certainly wouldn't get cramp. Yes, thought Mr Malt. It was definitely time for a swim.

Beside him, Mrs Malt sat up. 'Hello, dearest,' she said. She rubbed her eyes and yawned. 'Did you sleep well?'

'Very well. How about you?'

'I didn't sleep at all,' said Mrs Malt. 'I just dozed.' She looked around. 'Where's Tim?'

'I don't know.'

'You don't know?'

'I've been asleep,' said Mr Malt. 'So I haven't seen him. I suppose he must have gone for a walk.'

Mrs Malt looked worried. 'Do you think he'll be all right?'

'I'm sure he'll be fine.'

'I don't really like the idea of him wandering round a tropical island alone.'

'He's not alone,' said Mr Malt. 'He's with Grk. And I'm sure he'll be absolutely fine on this island. The only things that live here are gulls and turtles.'

'Even so, I think we should find him.' Mrs Malt stood up. She looked around. She called out, 'Tim? Timmy?' Then she shouted louder. 'TIM!'

There was no response.

Mrs Malt looked up and down the beach, staring at the white sand and the tall palm trees, but she couldn't see any sign of her son. A couple of birds flew overhead, their large wings flapping lazily as if they too preferred to spend the afternoons asleep.

'We'd better look for him,' said Mrs Malt. She didn't like the idea of her son – her only son, her only child – wandering around this strange island on his own. She felt furious with herself for falling asleep. She should have stayed awake to keep an eye on him. 'Terence, you go that way.' She pointed down the beach. 'And I'll go this way.'

'Yes, dear,' said Mr Malt in a weary voice. He stood up and started walking along the beach in the direction that Mrs Malt had indicated. He would have preferred to go swimming. He was sure that Tim was perfectly capable of looking after himself, particularly when he was accompanied by Grk. Tim was a sensible boy and Grk was an intelligent dog and the two of them wouldn't do anything stupid. But Mr Malt knew that there was no point arguing with his wife. He strolled along the sand. Every few steps, he shouted into the undergrowth, 'Tim! Tim!' But there was no answer.

Mr Malt had walked about fifty paces when he heard a shout.

'TERENCE!'

Mr Malt stopped and turned round.

His wife was standing at the other end of the beach. She shouted again. 'TERENCE!'

'Yes, dear,' said Mr Malt.

Mrs Malt waved at him. 'COME HERE!'

'Why?'

'JUST COME HERE!'

'Yes, dear.' Mr Malt hurried back along the beach, retracing his steps, until he reached his wife. 'How can I help?'

Mrs Malt pointed at some marks scrawled on the sand. 'What do you think this means?'

Mr Malt stood beside his wife. The marks, he saw, were actually words. He read them.

TOOK BOAT
BACK SOON
LOVE TIM

Mr Malt blinked and read them again. Then he laughed.

Mrs Malt stared at her husband in astonishment. She said, 'What's so funny?'

'That,' said Mr Malt, pointing at the words scrawled into the sand.

'What's funny about it?'

'It's terrifically funny. This is just Tim's idea of a joke. He's probably hiding in the undergrowth right now, watching us.'

'A joke?'

'Yes.'

'You think this is a joke?'

'Yes.'

'Then where's the boat?'

Mr Malt stared at his wife. 'The boat?'

'Yes, Terence. If this is a joke, then where is the boat?'

'The boat,' said Mr Malt. He lifted his head and stared at the bay. The water looked blue and clear and clean and completely empty. 'The boat,' he said once again, as if he had never heard the word before. 'The boat's gone.'

'Yes, dear. That's right. The boat has gone.'

'Where can it have gone?'

'Judging by this note, I would guess that Tim's taken it.'

'But he doesn't know how to drive a boat.'

'He *didn't* know how to drive a boat,' said Mrs Malt. 'Until this morning.'

'What happened this morning?'

'If you remember, Terence, you taught him exactly how to drive a boat. You showed him how to use the compass. You showed him how to use the throttle. You showed him how to use the steering wheel. Anyone would think that you'd deliberately taught him how to steal a boat and leave his parents abandoned on a tropical island in the middle of the Indian Ocean.'

'Of course I didn't do it deliberately,' said Mr Malt.

'It doesn't matter *why* you did it,' snapped Mrs Malt. 'What matters is that you *did* it. And now we're stuck here. On an island. In the middle of the ocean. Miles from anywhere. With no boat. And nothing to eat except three hard-boiled eggs.' Mrs Malt sighed. 'What are we going to do?'

'There's probably no need to worry,' said Mr Malt. 'He must have gone fishing. Or snorkelling. He's probably just taken the boat for a spin round the island. I'm sure he'll be back soon.'

Mrs Malt said, 'And what if he doesn't come back? What then? We'll be stuck on this island. With nothing to eat. And nowhere to sleep. And absolutely no way to contact the civilised world. Oh, this is terrible, Terence. This is just so terrible.'

Mr Malt said, 'Do you have your phone?'

'Of course I have my phone,' said Mrs Malt. She rummaged through her bag and found her mobile phone. She stared at the display, then shook her head. 'There's no signal.' She sighed. 'No one will ever know we're here. We could be stuck on this island for days.'

'It might be quite fun,' said Mr Malt.

'Fun?' Mrs Malt stared at her husband. 'Fun? Why on earth would that be fun?'

'You never know,' said Mr Malt.

'I do know,' said Mrs Malt. 'Being trapped on an island, miles from anywhere, with three boiled eggs and no toilet – that is not my idea of fun!'

Chapter 24

The black Zodiac roared through the waves, leaving a long white wake.

As you probably know, a Zodiac is a CRRC – a combat rubber raiding craft – and this particular model had been customised with twin engines, allowing it to move faster through the water than just about anything except a speedboat.

Three men sat inside the Zodiac. One controlled the outboard motor. The other two squatted at the front, searching the sea and the shore with their binoculars. All of them were wearing green army fatigues and carrying machine guns. The wind beat against their sunburnt faces.

Every hour, a Zodiac left the island's small harbour and drove once around the entire island, checking for intruders. Edward Goliath didn't want anyone or anything to disturb his solitude.

On their hourly patrols, the guards very rarely found anyone. You had to be lost or stupid to find yourself anywhere near Calypso Island, and probably both.

Once or twice a month, a patrol stumbled across a fishing boat from one of the other islands, searching for untapped stocks, which would turn around and flee as soon as the fishermen caught sight of the Zodiac. Or they would see a luxury yacht with some tourists at the helm who had thought it would be fun to try trespassing on a private island. The sight of three uniformed guards with machine guns was usually enough to send the tourists scurrying for the high seas. Firing a shot or two into the air always made them sail away even faster.

The Zodiac had travelled halfway round the island, just past the southernmost tip, when one of the guards shouted to the others. He had seen something through his binoculars. He pointed at the shore. 'Over there! There! You see?'

'What is it?'

'Looks like a boat,' yelled the guard. Then he shook his head. 'But it can't be a boat.'

'Why not?'

'Because it's halfway up a tree!'

'What are you talking about? Have you been drinking again?'

'Stop the engine,' said the guard. 'Have a look for yourself.'

The Zodiac slowed and stopped. The three guards stood up, lifted their binoculars to their eyes and stared at the shore.

Yes – there it was! All of them could see it now. A boat on the beach. But it wasn't anchored in the water or even pulled up onto the sand. It was wrapped around a palm tree.

Without a word, the three guards dropped back into the Zodiac and assumed their positions. They knew exactly what to do. They had practised many times for this event.

The first guard steered the Zodiac towards the shore at full speed. The second guard radioed to base, reporting the presence of an intruder and describing their precise position. The third guard knelt at the front of the Zodiac and put his gun to his shoulder. He placed his finger gently on the trigger and peered through the sights, scouring the shore, searching for any sign of a human presence. If he saw someone, he knew exactly what to do. Edward Goliath had given strict orders. Shoot first and ask questions later. This was a private island. Trespassers would be shot. The guard curled his finger around the trigger and smiled.

Chapter 25

Tim's head hurt. His legs hurt. His arms hurt. Even his eyes and his ears hurt. Everything hurt. He was sprawled on the floor in a tangle of limbs, aching all over. He couldn't remember how he came to be here or why. He couldn't think of anything except the pain.

Tim sat up.

That was a mistake. Now everything hurt even more. He clutched his skull with both hands and gently rubbed his scalp with the tips of his fingers.

The pain didn't go away.

There was something else too. He didn't just feel the pain. He could hear it. A strange buzzing noise echoed round his head, as if a bee had flown through his mouth and taken up residence inside his skull.

The last thing he remembered was seeing a big tree coming towards him at great speed.

Oh, yes. Now he remembered how he came to be lying here, covered in cuts and bruises. He knew what had happened.

The buzzing grew louder. It wasn't coming from inside his head. He hadn't swallowed a bee. Maybe a wasps' nest had fallen from the tree. Or perhaps petrol was hissing out of the tank onto the sand. Any second now, a spark would ignite the fumes. The boat would explode in a roar of flame.

Time to move, thought Tim. Time to get out of here.

The buzzing got louder every second.

Down at the other end of the cockpit, Grk was squatting on the floor, licking himself. He lifted his head, glanced at Tim for a moment, then went back to licking himself.

Tim stood up slowly. His legs hurt, his arms hurt and his head hurt. But he didn't fall over.

There was a loud noise behind him – a kind of whoosh or a whistle, followed by a loud bang.

He turned round, searching for the cause of the noise. There was another whoosh and another bang. A small hole appeared in the metal beside his head.

Tim stared at the hole. How had that happened? Holes can't just appear. Where did it come from?

And then it happened again. A whoosh. A bang. Another hole appeared in the metal. It was followed by another. And another. Until a line of holes ran along the cockpit and Tim realised that someone was shooting at him.

He ducked.

More bullets whistled overhead. Some smashed into the boat. Others thudded into the trunks of the surrounding palm trees or whistled into the jungle.

Someone was shooting at him. With bullets. Real bullets. And why?

It must be a mistake. A simple case of mistaken identity. They must think he was a thief or a bandit.

Tim knew that he had two options.

Option number one: he could surrender. He could stand up in the middle of the boat with his arms raised and hope they stopped shooting. He could beg for mercy. He could explain that someone, somewhere, had made a terrible mistake. He could ask why on earth anyone would want to shoot at a small boy and an even smaller dog.

Option number two: he could just run.

He just ran.

'Come on,' he yelled to Grk. 'Let's go! This way!'

Tim vaulted over the front of the boat and sprinted across the sand. Grk sprinted after him. Bullets sprayed the beach, pursuing them, creating little splashes of sand around their feet, pounding holes in the nearby tree trunks.

Tim's arms and legs still hurt. He was still covered in cuts and bruises. But that didn't stop him running as fast as he had ever run in his life. It's funny how fast you can run when someone is shooting at you.

Tim and Grk sprinted between the trunks of two huge palm trees. Blocking their way, there was a large white sign painted with black letters. Tim didn't have time to read what it said. He just sped round the side and charged into the forest. Grk ducked under the sign and ran after Tim.

Behind them, bullets sprayed the sand, the trees, the undergrowth and the sign, puncturing the white metal, peppering the black letters with a hundred holes. But the bullets didn't manage to destroy all the letters. If you had clambered up the sand after Tim, you still could have read what they said:

**TRESPASSERS
WILL BE
PROSECUTED**

The sign did not tell the truth, of course. The sign didn't say that trespassers would be shot. But Edward Goliath had not become one of the richest men on the planet by telling the truth.

Chapter 26

As the Zodiac approached the shore, the guard at the back cut the engine.

At the front of the Zodiac, the other two guards were poised to jump. They stared at the shore, searching the trees and the rocks. Any second now, they knew, a shot might ring out. Bullets might spray the air. They could be sailing straight into an ambush.

The three guards weren't quite sure what they had seen. When a Zodiac spurts through the sea at high speed, its nose lifts out of the water. It leaps over waves. And its passengers are thrown from side to side. So they can't aim their weapons or their binoculars. That was why the guard with the gun had been unable to plant a bullet between Tim's shoulder blades. And that was why the guard with the binoculars had been unable to spot exactly how many men had invaded the island. They didn't know if they were facing a dozy fisherman who had accidentally run his boat aground or a small army of pirates.

They dragged the Zodiac onto the beach and charged down the sand towards the red boat.

The guards stared at the boat. The windscreen was completely smashed. The hull had been gashed open. This boat wouldn't be going anywhere for a long time.

There was a sudden noise from the jungle.

The guards whirled round, raised their guns and fired

three streams of bullets into the trees.

Feathers fluttered through the air. Some broken branches fell from the trees and crashed to the ground, followed by a dead bird. But no one fired back.

One of the guards reached to his belt and removed a two-way radio. He switched it on. 'Alpha One,' he said. 'Alpha One, do you read me?'

Chapter 27

Tim knew the island was small, so he was careful not to run too far. He didn't want to emerge on the other side and find himself in a house, a barracks or a harbour, confronting more angry men with guns. He ran until he couldn't hear any more shots, then he ran a little more, and then he stopped in the middle of the jungle, surrounded by trees. He turned round and stared back at the way that he had come.

Grk sat at Tim's feet, watching Tim's face, waiting to see what he would do next.

They stayed absolutely still. It was quiet. He stood like that for a long time, listening for any unusual noise – a footstep, a shot or a breaking branch.

Around them, the jungle slowly came to life. Insects crawled along the ground. A butterfly dawdled through the air. A bright red bird flitted between the trees, a flash of scarlet against the green leaves, flying too fast for Tim to see any details.

But there was no sign or sound of humanity. No shots and no footsteps. They hadn't been followed.

Tim looked at Grk and said, 'So, what are we going to do now?'

Grk looked at Tim and wagged his tail. But he didn't offer any useful suggestions.

'I don't know which way to go,' said Tim. 'I don't even know what I should be looking for.'

Grk turned his head. He had smelled something interesting. He ran to the nearest tree and started sniffing the trunk.

Tim said, 'And without a boat, how are we going to get home?'

Grk didn't look up. He was too busy snuffling around the tree. He could smell something unusual. Something that he had never smelled before. He didn't know what it was, and he wasn't sure whether to be excited or terrified, but he kept sniffing, trying to locate the source of the smell.

'You're not a lot of help,' said Tim. He stared into the jungle. The foliage was dark and mysterious. All the trees looked the same. Tim didn't know which way to go. But anything would be better than returning to the beach and the bullets. He walked onwards.

Grk sniffed the trunk once more, then ran ahead, charging past Tim and darting ahead through the trees. He jumped over leaves and branches, then stopped and turned, his ears cocked, waiting for Tim to catch up.

Chapter 28

Edward Goliath's face was flushed bright red with fury. He had been listening to Toby Connaught's explanation for two minutes and he'd had enough. 'I don't understand,' he yelled, 'How did this happen? How did a boat get anywhere near the island – let alone crash on the beach?'

That afternoon, just like every afternoon, Edward Goliath was doing his afternoon exercises, watched by his doctor, his trainer and his nutritionist. The three of them flew round the world with him, going wherever he went, keeping him just about as healthy as it was possible for a sixty-one-year-old man to be. They monitored his heartbeat, his respiration and all his other vital statistics as he jogged, cycled, ran, swam and worked through the machines in his private gym.

But on that particular afternoon, unlike most afternoons, Goliath's exercises had been interrupted by the arrival of Toby Connaught, who had brought some bad news. A boat had been found on the other side of the island. The boat's occupants had vanished.

The doctor, the trainer and the nutritionist took several steps backwards. Each of them shook their heads. Calm down, they wanted to say. Take a deep breath. If you make yourself so angry, you'll burst a blood vessel. You might even have a heart attack. But none of them said a word, not daring to interrupt their boss.

The only person who dared speak was Toby Connaught. He said, 'We don't exactly know how the boat got here.'

'You don't know?'

'No, sir.'

'What do you mean? How can you not know?'

'There must have been a breach of the security systems.'

'A breach? What kind of breach?'

'They must have come under the radar, sir. And avoided the patrols. And sneaked past the cameras. They must be using extremely sophisticated equipment.'

'This is ridiculous,' said Goliath. 'Where are they now?'

'We don't know, sir.'

'And how many of them are there?'

'We don't know that either, sir.'

'Well, what do you know?'

'Not a lot, sir.' Quickly, Toby Connaught explained what the patrol had found on the beach on the other side of the island. He described the smashed boat and the figures who had been glimpsed fleeing from the beach to the jungle. He explained that the intruders couldn't have got far, because the guards had radioed their report only a couple of minutes ago. He promised that they could not remain undiscovered for long.

'Mobilise everyone,' said Goliath. 'Search the entire island. I want them found right now.'

Chapter 29

Tim and Grk had been walking through the jungle for a few minutes, hopping over fallen branches and weaving through the trees, when they stumbled onto a road.

Before Tim could choose whether to turn left or right, or plunge onwards through the jungle, the decision was made for him. He heard the noise of an engine. A car was coming. He jumped back and hid behind a tree.

Grk sat in the middle of the road, scratching his left ear with his right leg.

Tim whistled. 'Hey! Come here!'

Grk rolled over and scratched his right ear with his left leg.

The noise of the engine was getting louder. The car must be just around the corner.

Tim clapped his hands. 'Come on, Grk! Come here!'

Grk looked up. For a moment, he seemed to be considering which of his ears still needed scratching. Then he must have remembered that he had already scratched both of them, because he bounded across the road and ran to Tim.

Just as Grk jumped out of the road and disappeared into the jungle, a jeep came racing round the corner. Tim kept perfectly still. He hoped Grk hadn't been seen.

There were three men in the jeep. One was driving. The others had binoculars slung around their necks and machine guns in their laps. The jeep whizzed down the road and skidded round the bend.

When the noise of the engine had faded, Tim stepped out of the undergrowth. Grk followed him. Tim looked up and down the road. Grk sniffed the air. When both of them were satisfied that the guards had gone and were not coming back, they started walking along the road, taking the opposite direction from the jeep.

After a few minutes, they reached a clearing in the jungle. Tim could see a single-storey brick building with a flat roof. Two jeeps and three bicycles were parked beside the building, but there was no sign of any people.

Tim stayed very still, watching and listening. He didn't want to take any risks.

When he was satisfied that the clearing was empty, he walked slowly forwards, turning his head all the time, looking in every direction, checking for guards.

Tim decided that he must be right in the middle of the island, because he couldn't hear the sea. Overhead, the sky was blue, studded with wispy white clouds. The long single-storey building stood at one edge of the clearing. It had a wooden door.

On the other side of the clearing there were three large green rocks.

Grk ran towards the nearest rock.

'Not that way,' hissed Tim. 'This way!'

Grk glanced at Tim, then continued running towards the rock.

'Come back!' Tim wanted to look at the building, and peer through the window to see what was inside. He wasn't interested in large green rocks. 'Come on, Grk! Here!'

Grk took no notice. He reached the rock and sniffed it.

'Right, that's it,' said Tim. 'I'm putting you on the lead.' He reached into his pocket, pulled out Grk's lead and ran across the clearing.

He reached Grk. But before he could attach the lead to Grk's collar, something unexpected happened.

The rock twitched.

Tim stared. Grk jumped backwards. Neither of them had ever seen a twitching rock.

The rock twitched again.

A foot slid out from the bottom of the rock, followed almost immediately by a second foot.

A long neck emerged from the other side of the rock.

At the end of the neck, there was a large wrinkled head which turned slowly towards Tim and Grk. Two big black eyes stared at them with a quizzical expression.

Tim and Grk stared back. Neither of them had ever seen such an extraordinary creature.

It was an enormous tortoise.

Tim didn't know much about tortoises, but there was one thing that he knew for sure. This was the biggest tortoise that he had ever seen. He had never even imagined that such a huge tortoise existed anywhere on the planet.

The enormous tortoise had thick skin, wide legs, a huge shell, a long bendy neck and a big bulbous head. Its eyes were dark and mysterious.

Tim had always thought of tortoises as small creatures which lived in people's back gardens and hibernated in cardboard boxes during the winter. But here was an enormous tortoise – a tortoise as big as an armchair.

He didn't know if enormous tortoises had poisonous fangs or sharp teeth or long claws. He didn't know if they were bloodthirsty carnivores or kind-hearted vegetarians. He didn't know if they ate grass or leaves or worms or dogs or boys. Whatever their dietary habits, he couldn't imagine how they would react to the unexpected arrival of a boy and a dog, and he wasn't sure that he wanted to find out.

But Grk seemed quite intrigued. He wanted to know more about this curious creature. His tail wagged slowly back and forth.

The tortoise bent his head towards the ground.

Grk lifted his nose and sniffed the tortoise's wrinkled skin.

Tim turned his head. He could hear something. He listened out for a second, then identified the noise. It was an engine. The jeep was coming back.

This time, he didn't take any chances. The noise of the engine was quickly getting louder. Tim didn't want to get trapped between the soldiers and the tortoises. He attached the lead to Grk's collar and pulled him towards the trees.

Grk reluctantly followed Tim, turning his head every few paces to turn and stare at the tortoise.

The tortoise stared back.

Chapter 30

Tim and Grk lurked behind a large palm tree, peering round the side of the trunk. The noise of the approaching engine grew louder. A jeep emerged into the clearing. Two men in white coats sat in the two front seats. They looked like scientists.

They parked the jeep and switched off the engine. In the silence, Tim could hear the sound of his own breathing and Grk's panting.

The two scientists left their jeep and walked across the grass to the nearest tortoise. Both men leaned down to inspect it. The first scientist tapped the tortoise's shell. The second scientist touched the tortoise's skull. They spoke a few words to one another, then walked to the next tortoise and inspected that too.

When the two scientists had made their inspections of the tortoises, they turned round. Tim was worried that they might have seen him, but they hadn't. They walked across the grass to the single-storey building, opened the door and went inside. The door swung shut after them.

Tim waited for a couple of minutes, making sure that the two men weren't going to come straight out again, then darted towards the building. Grk ran after him.

When Tim reached the building, he ran past the door and continued to the nearest window. Ducking down to the ground, he waited to catch his breath, then very slowly raised his body until his eyes were at the level of the windowsill. He peered through the murky glass.

On the other side of the window he could see a large room, running the whole length of the building. Apart from several silver cabinets lined along one wall, the room appeared to be empty.

That wasn't possible. The room couldn't be empty. Two men had just walked inside and hadn't come out. They must be tucked away at one end of the building or the other, hidden from view.

Tim put his face against the glass. He peered to the left, then the right. He couldn't see anyone. As far as he could tell, the room was completely empty.

Tim was baffled. If the two scientists weren't inside the room, where had they gone?

'Come on,' he hissed to Grk. 'This way.'

Together, they hurried all the way round the building, checking for exits. Two walls were blank. On the third wall, there was a door – the door which the two men had gone through. And on the fourth, there was a window – the window that Tim had been looking through.

He looked through the window again. Nothing had changed. The room was still empty.

It just didn't make sense. Tim had been watching the door and the two men hadn't emerged. They must still be inside. But they weren't inside. They had vanished.

But two men can't just vanish.

Can they?

Tim walked round the building and stood beside the door, followed by Grk. He lifted his hand and wrapped his fingers around the handle. For a moment, he did nothing, unwilling to turn the handle, uncertain what he

113

might find on the other side of the door, worried that he was making a terrible mistake. Right now, he could just walk away. Or he could hide among the trees and wait for the men to emerge. Or he could turn the handle and go inside the building.

Forcing himself to move, not allowing himself the opportunity to change his mind, he turned the handle. The door wasn't locked. It opened immediately.

He knew he was being foolish, but curiosity drove him forwards. He had the strange sense that a secret was here inside this building, waiting to be exposed. If he went through this door, he felt certain, he would discover why Monsieur X had died. He would learn what Monsieur X's last words had meant. He would solve the mystery of Calypso Island.

Tim paused for a moment, giving himself one last chance to turn and run. He waited for a raised voice, the angry shout of someone demanding to know what he was doing, but nothing came.

Here goes, thought Tim.

He stepped inside the building. Grk followed him. The door swung shut behind them.

Chapter 31

Tim and Grk were standing at the end of a long room. One wall was lined with metal cupboards, another wall was punctuated by a single window and the third wall was blank. Apart from the cupboards, the room was empty. There was no sign of the two scientists.

Tim looked at Grk. He said, 'What do we do now?'

Grk didn't answer. He was sniffing the air, trying to identify a curious smell.

'You're not much help,' said Tim.

Grk just kept sniffing. There was something in the room which intrigued him. He ambled to the nearest wall and ran his nose along the floorboards, sniffing every knot and crevice.

Tim looked round the room, searching for some sign of the two scientists, something to convince him that he hadn't simply dreamed their presence, but he couldn't see anything. Perhaps I'm going mad, thought Tim. Perhaps I simply imagined them. He couldn't think of any other explanation. Two men can't simply walk into a room and then disappear. That's just not possible.

He stared at the cupboards. Could the scientists be hiding inside them? The cupboards stretched from the floor to the ceiling. Each one was wide enough to hold a human. But why would anyone choose to hide inside a cupboard?

There was only one way to find out. Tim stretched out

his arm, grabbed the handle on the nearest cupboard and opened it.

The door swung open. Cold air rushed out. The cupboard was a fridge.

Inside, there were three shelves, stacked with what looked like white balls. They were the size and shape of tennis balls. What were they? Tim could imagine all sorts of possibilities. They might have been bombs. They might have been candy-coated chocolate puddings. They might have been tiny croquet balls or massive golf balls. Whatever they were, it was obviously important to keep them at a steady temperature, because each shelf had its own thermometer.

Tim leaned forward. Gingerly, using both hands, he picked up one of the balls. It was cold and light and a little bit squishy. He knew immediately what it was.

An egg.

A white egg.

They weren't chicken eggs. They were too white and too round. Although he couldn't be certain, he guessed they must be tortoise eggs. Perhaps this was a laboratory devoted to studying tortoises and the two men in white coats really had been scientists, devoting their lives to saving giant tortoises from extinction.

Tim suddenly felt guilty. He realised that he might easily have made a terrible mistake. If the men who worked here were conservationists and environmentalists, they were the good guys. He didn't want to be caught sneaking around their laboratory. They might think he was trying to harm their work.

Tim put the egg back on the shelf and closed the door. He didn't want to damage the eggs.

He felt depressed. He had failed to find what he was looking for. He had been hoping to uncover traces of criminal activity, but this building seemed like a scientific research centre, devoted to saving tortoises.

For a moment, Tim considered walking out.

Then he decided to do one last thing. He would look inside the other fridges. If they contained more eggs, just like the first one, he would know that he had been wrong to come here.

He walked down the room to the next fridge, opened the door and quickly peeked inside. He saw another three shelves stacked with eggs. He shut the door again, not wanting to damage the eggs by altering their temperature.

He went along the line of fridges, opening every door. Five of the six cupboards were exactly the same. Each contained three shelves stacked with white eggs. Altogether, there must have been several hundred eggs crammed inside five fridges, enough to populate an entire town of tortoises.

But the sixth cupboard was different.

When Tim opened the door of the sixth cupboard, he didn't feel a blast of cold air or see a row of shelves, stacked with eggs. Instead, he saw an empty box, much like a cupboard without any shelves. The walls of this particular cupboard were made of shiny reflective metal. On the left-hand wall, there were two buttons, one above the other. The uppermost button was blue and the lower button was red.

It might have been an empty space, waiting for a fridge to be fitted inside.

Or, Tim thought, it might be something else completely.

Looking at the two buttons, the red and the blue, he had an idea what it might be.

There was only one way to test his idea and see if he was right. He stepped into the cupboard, pulled Grk after him, and let the door swing shut. Now they were trapped inside the cupboard. In each of the four gleaming walls, Tim could see himself reflected again and again, back and forth, surrounding him with infinite versions of himself and Grk.

Grk didn't appear to be interested in the mirrors and definitely disliked the sensation of being trapped. His tail drooped. His ears flattened on the back of his head. He looked at Tim with a mournful expression which seemed to say something like, 'Can we get out of here?'

'In a minute,' said Tim. 'First, I have to try something. If it doesn't work, then we can get out of here.'

Grk's tail drooped even further.

Tim pressed the uppermost button, the blue one.

Nothing happened.

He pressed the blue button again and still nothing happened.

He pressed the lower button, the red one.

Immediately, his stomach lurched. Grk whined in terror. The metal cupboard was moving downwards.

As Tim had suspected, they were standing in a small lift. It plunged down, down, down towards the centre of the earth.

Chapter 32

The lift stopped suddenly. The door slid open. Tim walked out. Grk hurried after him.

They found themselves standing in a long, empty corridor, lit with a strange yellowish glow. They must have been deep underground, but the air was cool and fresh. There was a curious humming sound which didn't seem to come from any particular direction.

Grk lifted his nose into the air and sniffed. He could smell something strange, something unexpected. The hair on his neck flattened and he uttered a low, ominous growl.

Tim looked down at Grk. 'What's wrong?'

Grk growled once more, then lifted his head and looked at Tim with unhappy eyes. He didn't like this place, he seemed to be saying. He wanted to get out of here. Right now.

Tim whispered, 'What is it? What's wrong?'

In response, Grk took a couple of steps towards the lift, then looked back at Tim. Let's go, he seemed to be saying. Let's get back in the lift and escape from here. This isn't a good place.

'I don't like it either,' whispered Tim. 'But we've come all this way. We can't leave now. Come on, Grk. This way.'

He took a few paces down the corridor, then stopped and looked back. Grk hadn't followed him.

'Come on,' hissed Tim, tugging the lead. 'Let's go!'

Reluctantly, Grk trotted after Tim.

Together, they walked down the long, white corridor. Tim went ahead. Grk followed a few paces behind, his ears flat against the back of his head, his whole body expressing anxiety.

Tim had never seen Grk look so frightened. In fact, Tim couldn't remember ever having seen Grk looking frightened at all. Hungry, yes. Tired, yes. Cross, yes. But frightened? No, fear was not an emotion that Grk allowed himself to feel. And so Tim couldn't help feeling a little bit frightened too, just as he couldn't help wondering what Grk could sense or smell that caused him to feel such fear.

At the end of the corridor, there was a steel door with two buttons, a red one and a blue one. Tim pressed the red button and the door slid open. Immediately, a strong smell wafted through the air, something like a mixture between sewage and rotten vegetables. It reminded Tim of a place that he had visited recently, but he couldn't think where.

The door slid shut behind them.

They were standing on a narrow steel platform. Ahead, there was a handrail at about the height of Tim's chest. To the left and right, the platform ran around the length of the wall.

Tim took a few steps forward, leaned on the handrail and looked down. Grk shuffled after him.

The platform was high above the ground. To his amazement, Tim realised that they must be inside an enormous cave, carved from the heart of the island.

120

Overhead, specks of water dribbled through cracks in the bare rock and dropped fifty metres to the floor below.

A network of steel walkways and staircases criss-crossed the cavern. At regular intervals along the walls, there were dark entrances, some barricaded by bars and others blocked by solid steel doors.

Down on the ground, Tim could see strange assemblies of complex machinery, covered with levers and tubes. There was a small crane and a row of electronic microscopes and the type of operating table that you might find in a doctor's surgery. Twenty computers squatted on low tables. A tower of cages held about a hundred white mice.

There was no natural light or ventilation. Fluorescent bulbs provided a pale yellowish glow which made everything, even Tim's skin and Grk's fur, look curiously artificial.

Now Tim understood the source of the continuous humming that he could hear; that must be the sound of air conditioning, pumping fresh air from the surface into this contained space.

The smell seemed stronger now, but Tim still couldn't remember where he had smelled it before.

Tim couldn't see any people, or even signs of life, but the cavern was full of peculiar sounds, groans and yells, mewling and moaning, a kind of growl and the songs of exotic birds, as if someone had recorded the sounds of a kennel and a cattery and a forest and a jungle, and was now playing the soundtrack over and over again, mingling all the noises of different animals together.

121

Tim couldn't begin to imagine how much time, effort and money must have been spent to create this place, but he could immediately imagine why the island's owner would have done so. Nowhere else on the entire planet could possibly be so private. Buried underground on a private island, hidden from intruders and prying eyes, this cavern would be entirely secret. Even spy planes or satellites wouldn't be able to see what was happening here. If you wanted to do something completely confidential – and, perhaps, illegal – then you couldn't create a better environment than this.

Grk barked twice, loudly.

'Shh,' hissed Tim.

But Grk took no notice. His tail was wagging and his ears had perked up. He barked again, twice more, louder.

From the other side of the cavern, an answering bark came back. For a moment, Tim assumed that the bark must have been just an echo of Grk's, bouncing back from the opposite wall, but then it was joined by another and another and another, each bark different from the others, none quite the same as Grk's. Somewhere in this enormous cavern, hidden down a corridor or roaming along the walkways, there must be some dogs.

Guard dogs, thought Tim. Ferocious guard dogs with strong jaws and sharp teeth. They will run along these steel walkways and rip us to pieces. He looked around, searching for an escape route, trying to decide which way to run. To the left and the right, the walkway looked exactly the same, running alongside the bare rock.

Before Tim could decide whether to run to the left or

the right, the noise of barking was joined by other, stranger noises, the roars and groans of twenty different animals, jumbled together, swelling out of the cavern and echoing around the vast rocky roof.

Tim guessed that the noise must be playing through loudspeakers. Perhaps it was designed to scare intruders. Perhaps someone was making a film. Or perhaps... and then, as Tim tried to think of further explanations, he suddenly realised where he had smelled the distinctive stench that pervaded the air. Last December, during the dull period between Christmas and New Year, his parents had taken him to London Zoo.

Before Tim could begin to imagine why or how the cavern smelled like a zoo, he saw two men emerging from a doorway. They strolled along the cavern's floor. They were wearing khaki uniforms and black boots. They had machine guns slung over their shoulders.

Tim kept very still, knowing that any sudden movement might attract their attention. But if they didn't look up, they wouldn't see him.

On the opposite side of the cavern, a door slid open and two more men emerged. Rather than uniforms, these two were wearing long white coats. From here, high above them, Tim couldn't see their faces, but they might have been the scientists that he had seen earlier.

Down in the middle of the cavern's floor, the four men met and talked. None of them looked upwards at the steel walkways running round the top of the cavern. None of them noticed a small boy, lurking in the middle of the highest walkway, leaning on the handrail, standing very still, hoping not to be seen.

The four men talked for a couple of minutes. Around them, the noises of angry, terrified animals – mewling, groaning, gibbering, moaning – gradually subsided until the cavern was so quiet that Tim could almost distinguish the actual words that the four men were speaking.

The guards continued walking. The scientists sat at separate tables and started working on computers. Tim watched them for a moment, then tugged Grk's lead. 'This way,' he whispered, his voice so quiet that he couldn't even hear himself.

Grk stared at Tim, making no secret of his reluctance. His ears were flattened against his skull and his tail was down. He didn't like this place. He didn't want to stay here another second. He would have preferred to walk back down the corridor to the lift and return to the surface. But he didn't have any choice. One end of a lead was tied to his collar and the other was in Tim's hand. Slowly, Grk padded after Tim. Together, the boy and the dog headed along the metal walkway.

Chapter 33

Tim tried to walk quietly. He knew that if his footsteps resounded against the metal walkway, the guards or the scientists might hear him. He tiptoed down a flight of stairs, followed by Grk, and continued along the next walkway. Every few paces, he passed another doorway. He glanced into each one and saw a variety of different rooms. Most were empty. A few contained the sort of equipment that you might see in a doctor's or dentist's surgery – forceps, clamps, drills, drips, operating tables and syringes. Others contained apparatus that looked unlike anything that Tim had ever seen before. He couldn't imagine what happened in this cavern. He couldn't make sense of all the different things that he had seen.

As he passed the tenth or twelfth doorway, he glanced inside and saw a sight so surprising that he stopped, unable to take another step.

The doorway was blocked by a mesh of strong, slim metal bars. On the other side, there was a cave carved out of the rock, making a cell that was probably no bigger than your kitchen and perhaps a little smaller. Inside the cell, there was a tiger.

The tiger was so still that Tim thought it must be made of plastic. Then he realised that the tiger's chest was rising and falling with each slow, steady breath.

The tiger wasn't made of plastic. She was just utterly depressed.

Tigers need space. They are ferocious, energetic animals which roam for miles through the jungle, searching for food. But this particular tiger had been confined to a small cave for a long, long time and lost her love of life. Confinement had sapped her energy and ferocity. Her eyes were dull and watery. Fur had fallen from her body, leaving patches of bald skin. The tiger lay on the ground, unable even to rouse enough strength to lift her head and peer at the boy and the dog lingering outside her cell.

Tim and Grk stared at the tiger for a couple of minutes, then continued along the walkway.

In the next cell, they saw a goat lying on a patch of straw, munching slowly and contentedly.

In the cell after that, they saw three monkeys, slumped on the floor like old men exhausted by a heavy meal.

The following three cells contained a sheep, several rabbits and a giant tortoise, just like the one that Tim had seen on the surface.

Now Tim understood the source of the smell. The cavern smelled like a zoo because it was a zoo.

But why would Edward Goliath keep a zoo down here? Why would he confine his animals to small cells, far underground, rather than letting them roam on the island's surface?

Tim and Grk continued walking.

In the next cell, they found a creature that Tim had never expected to see in a zoo. Behind the bars, there was a man.

Just like the other animals in the zoo, the man was sitting on the floor of an empty cage. He looked thin and weak. He had straggly white hair which hung about his face. He was wearing faded blue jeans and a white shirt. His feet were bare.

The man lifted his head and stared at Tim. In his bloodshot eyes, there was an expression of overwhelming boredom and despair.

Tim stared back for a second, then hurried onwards, unable to meet the man's eyes for more than a second.

As he continued along the walkway, he wondered whether he should go back again and do something – talk to the man, perhaps, or try to free him.

But he couldn't bring himself to turn round. He didn't want to look into those eyes again.

Grk was right. This was a bad place. Whatever was happening here, Tim didn't like it.

He hurried past more cells. Each was barricaded by steel bars. Each contained a human being. There were three men and one woman. All of them seemed terrified of Tim. The woman covered her head with both hands as if she was trying to protect herself from a punch. The men shuffled backwards, putting as much distance as possible between themselves and the doorway. None of them even attempted to speak.

The next cell held something that Tim had never seen before and never even imagined in his most horrible nightmares, a creature that was neither human nor tortoise, but a bit of both. It was a giant tortoise with a human hand growing from the top of its shell, the fingers lifting upwards as if they were reaching for the sky.

Tim and Grk stood outside the cell and stared through the bars.

The tortoise stared back. It opened its mouth and made a low moaning noise.

Tim couldn't look. He turned his head away and walked along the line of cells.

In the final cell before the staircase, there was a tortoise with three ears grafted into its shell.

Human ears.

Three human ears surgically attached to the shell of a giant tortoise.

Tim felt sick. He had never seen anything so disgusting.

He tried to imagine what kind of person might do this – and, just as importantly, why they would possibly want to do this. But he couldn't. It was beyond the powers of his imagination.

He looked down at Grk.

Grk looked up at him with small, frightened eyes.

You're right to be scared, thought Tim. I'm scared too.

Now he wished that he'd taken more notice of Grk.

Grk had tried to escape from this place, not wishing to spend a single second longer here than he had to. As always, Grk had been right. It would have been better to leave this place immediately.

Tim turned round, tugged Grk's lead and hurried back the way that they had come. Grk trotted alongside him, pleased to be leaving.

They walked past the tortoises and the humans and the horrific creatures that were both tortoise and human, then climbed the stairs to the next level.

And then they stopped.

Two men were coming towards them. Two men

wearing khaki uniforms and carrying machine guns.

For a moment, the four of them – the guards and the boy and the dog – stared at one another, too surprised to move or speak. Then, one of the men shouted and the other raised his gun. Tim and Grk turned and ran back down the stairs.

They sprinted along the walkway, reached another flight of stairs, and ran down those too.

They were on the lowest level. They ran across the floor, heading for the other side. Tim barely had time to register what he was running past. He noticed a bank of computers, a tray of gleaming medical implements and some kind of enormous table, covered with straps and tubes.

On the other side of the cavern, there were two brightly-lit corridors leading into the rock. Tim wavered for a moment, trying to decide whether to go left or right. Before he could make a decision, a guard stepped out of each corridor.

Tim turned round.

From the other way, more guards were approaching.

There was no escape.

The guards surrounded Tim and Grk. One spoke into a two-way radio. Another stepped forward and shouted in a language that Tim couldn't understand.

'I'm terribly sorry,' said Tim. 'But I've got no idea what you're saying. Do you speak English?'

In strongly-accented English, the guard said, 'You put your hands in the air! Right now!'

Very slowly, Tim raised his hands into the air.

Chapter 34

For several hours, Mr and Mrs Malt had not exchanged a single word.

They could have been talking to one another. They were both on the same beach. There was no one else available for conversation. But Mrs Malt had been sitting by the sea and Mr Malt had been standing by the trees and not a word had passed between them.

Mr Malt had not been idle. In fact, he'd been working extremely hard. He had paced along the line of trees, searching for the perfect spot. He wanted somewhere sheltered from the wind and shadowed from the sun, yet within sight of the sea. He soon found an ideal clearing between two tall palms.

He walked around the site, inspecting it from every angle, then retreated a few paces down the beach and stood with his arms folded over his chest, picturing exactly what he wanted to build. When he had a firm vision in his mind, he hurried into the woods and hunted through the trees, gathering branches, twigs and leaves.

When Mr Malt finished building his shelter, just before sunset, he walked down the beach. He found his wife sitting on the sand, staring at the sea. She had her head in her hands.

'Hello,' said Mr Malt.

His wife did not reply.

Mr Malt spread his arms to encompass the view – the rosy sky, the azure waves, the white sand, the palm trees. He said, 'Isn't this lovely?'

Mrs Malt still didn't respond. She didn't even move. Her head stayed resolutely clasped in her hands.

Mr Malt said, 'Melanie?'

There was no response.

Mr Malt said, 'Are you all right?'

There was still no response.

Mr Malt said, 'We should probably start thinking about supper.'

Finally, Mrs Malt lifted her head, turned and looked at her husband. 'Supper,' she said in a low voice. 'Oh, yes. Supper. So, what shall we have for supper? A nice steak? Some roast chicken? Or how about another plate of that delicious foie gras?'

'We've got three boiled eggs,' said Mr Malt. 'That's one and a half each. Plus an apple and a cucumber.'

'Terrific,' said Mrs Malt. 'When you were having your jolly holidays in Devon, I don't suppose you learned how to catch a fish?'

'No, but I have managed to find some fruit which looks rather interesting. It was growing on a tree in the jungle. The only thing is, I have no idea if it's poisonous.'

'Why don't you try some,' said Mrs Malt. 'If you're still alive in a week, we'll know it's not poisonous.'

Mr Malt sighed. 'You seem a bit angry with me,' he said. 'I don't think that's entirely fair.'

'Angry? Really? I'm so sorry if I seem angry. But I'm not exactly having the best holiday of my life.'

131

'Nor am I. But that's no reason to be angry with me. It's not my fault.'

'Terence, who stole the boat?'

'Tim did.'

'And who taught him to drive a boat?'

'That's not fair,' said Mr Malt. 'You can't blame me for what Tim did.'

'I can blame you,' said Mrs Malt. 'And I do.' With that, she turned her back on her husband and returned to staring at the ocean.

Mr Malt looked at the back of his wife's head for a few moments. Then he sighed. There were many things that he could have said, but he thought it was probably wisest to say none of them. He slouched slowly back up the beach. As he walked, he gathered a couple of branches. They would do very well for the doorway.

Halfway up the beach, he stopped for a moment and contemplated his shelter. Although he said so himself, it looked extremely professional. Not many castaways could have built themselves such good shelters on their first night. He was very pleased with his own skill and ingenuity.

He remembered the books that he had read as a boy. *Robinson Crusoe. Bevis. Treasure Island. Swallows and Amazons.* He remembered all the different heroes that he had admired so much. Peter and Bevis and Jim and Robinson himself. Did any of them have to cope with a depressed wife? No, they did not. They had troubles of their own, of course. No one would deny that. They had to struggle against pirates and hunger and storms. Even so, he would have liked to see how Peter, Bevis, Jim or

Robinson dealt with Melanie Malt.

When Mr Malt reached his shelter, he propped the two branches in the doorway. Just as he had hoped, they fitted perfectly.

Mr Malt sat in the doorway of his shelter and carefully separated his share of the remaining food. He halved the apple, the cucumber and one of the eggs. He ate his halves, putting the remainder aside for Melanie. He knew what she was like. She might be grumpy now, but she would get hungry later.

As he ate, he tried to savour every mouthful, knowing that he might not eat again for several hours or even days.

When he had eaten, he went for a pee among the trees, then walked down to the sea and washed his hands, face and feet. He glanced along the beach. His wife was sitting exactly where he had left her. He didn't disturb her.

He walked back up the beach, undressed and clambered inside the shelter. The blanket of palm leaves was surprisingly comfortable. Mr Malt stretched out. A few minutes later, he was asleep.

In the middle of the night, Mr Malt was woken by a strange rustling. He had visions of panthers searching for a midnight feast. He imagined lizards gobbling his feet. And then he realised that Mrs Malt had crawled into the shelter beside him.

Mr Malt sat up and rubbed his eyes. In a bleary voice, he said, 'Are you hungry? Do you want the other egg?'

Without a word, Mrs Malt lay down and turned her back on her husband.

Mr Malt stared through the gloom at his wife's back. He would have liked to say something, but he couldn't think of anything to say. So he lay down and closed his eyes.

Chapter 35

At the entrance to the tunnel, there was a railway wagon with eight small wheels, sitting on a pair of metal tracks.

The guards ushered Tim into the wagon. He sat on one of the slim wooden benches. Grk lay on the floor at his feet. A guard sat on either side of Tim. Another two sat opposite. The fifth pressed a button. The wagon shuddered forward, then started speeding along the tracks. It went surprisingly fast. The breeze whooshed through their hair.

The tunnel ran from the cavern to the surface. When the builders had been excavating the cavern, they used these tracks to remove debris. Once the cavern was built, the tracks carried cages, computers and animals into the laboratories.

They had been moving for a couple of minutes when, up ahead, a pair of doors swung open automatically. The tracks ran out of the tunnel and continued down the length of the quay, then a switch clicked and the wagon rolled to a halt.

Emerging from the dimly-lit tunnel into the bright sunshine, Tim and the guards shaded their eyes, blinking at the sudden contrast. Grk strained at the lead, eager to jump out of the wagon, wanting to sniff the sea and the salt and the fish and the seaweed and all the other interesting smells clamouring to be smelled.

The wagon had come to a halt at the edge of a small

harbour. Edward Goliath owned several boats which were moored against the quays – six powerful speed-boats, a pair of small yachts and a massive white cruiser. Tim could read the name written in flowing black letters on the hull: *The Fountain of Youth*.

Tim hardly had time to admire the beautiful boats, their polished decks gleaming in the sunlight, before he was hurried towards a stairway cut into the rock, leading from the harbour to the house on the cliff. Two guards walked ahead of him and two more behind.

At the top of the stairway, the guards ushered Tim and Grk along a gravel path. Heavily scented flowers filled the air with sweet smells. Oranges, lemons and mangoes hung from trees. They passed a long swimming pool and two tennis courts before reaching the house.

Several more guards were waiting. All of them were dressed in the same way, wearing khaki uniforms, black boots and peaked caps.

They led him into the house. It was a luxurious mansion which felt more like a hotel than a home. Vases of fresh flowers rested on polished wooden tables. Large abstract paintings graced the walls.

They walked down several corridors, then came to a door. A guard knocked twice and said something in a language that Tim couldn't understand. There was an answering shout in English: 'Send him in!'

The guard opened the door and pushed Tim inside. Grk scampered after him. The door swung shut behind them and closed with an almost inaudible click.

Tim found himself standing at the end of a long, high-ceilinged room with big windows overlooking the ocean. This could have been a dining room or a meeting room. There was a long wooden table surrounded by twenty chairs. Down at the end of the table, a single place was laid for dinner.

A tall, handsome man was walking towards Tim. He had a strong chin and tanned skin. He was wearing shorts, trainers and a bright blue shirt. 'Ah-hah!' he said, clapping his hands together enthusiastically. 'So you're the little trespasser. Is that right?'

'I suppose I must be,' said Tim.

The man smiled, showing two lines of white, gleaming, perfect teeth. 'Welcome to Calypso,' he said. 'My name is Edward Goliath.' He spread his arms wide to encompass the room. 'This is my house. In fact, this is my island.' Goliath took a long look at the boy who was standing before him. 'And what's your name?'

'Tim.'

'Just Tim? Or do you have another name too?'

'Malt. My name is Timothy Malt.'

'Hello, Timothy Malt,' said Goliath. He looked at the dog standing by Tim's feet. 'And this is?'

'Grk,' said Tim.

Hearing his name, Grk wagged his tail and barked twice.

Goliath said, 'So, Tim, you and your dog have caused me a certain amount of trouble. Do you know that?'

Tim said, 'I suppose so.'

'Will you tell me what you're doing here – and why you crashed a boat on my island?'

'I came to see what happened to Monsieur X.'

'Monsieur X? Who might he be?'

'The man who was washed up on the beach,' said Tim.

137

Goliath nodded. 'Ah, yes. That man. Now, I understand. You are the little boy who found him, are you?'

'Yes,' said Tim.

'And you think he had some connection to this island?'

'I know he did,' said Tim.

'You know he did? Do you? And how exactly do you know that?'

Tim didn't actually know very much at all, but he had guessed what had happened to Monsieur X and he was almost certain that his guesswork was correct. 'You kept him prisoner, but he escaped. He was so desperate to get away, he threw himself into the sea and tried to swim away. But he couldn't swim all the way to Mahé. He was half dead by the time he got there.'

'You're a clever boy,' said Goliath, putting his hand on Tim's shoulder. 'Come over here. Sit down. You and I should have a little chat.'

They walked to the table. Goliath sat at the head, where a single place had been laid for dinner.

'Sit down here,' said Goliath, gesturing at the place beside him, the one without plates or cutlery.

Tim sat down. Grk sniffed the table leg a few times, then lay down at Tim's feet.

Tim was hungry, so he was pleased to see that there wasn't any food on the table. It might have been unbearable to stare at food that he couldn't eat. Beside Goliath's place, a place was set for one person. There was chunky silver cutlery, an elegant white plate and several little silver pots for salt, pepper, mustard and relish.

Goliath said, 'Will you have a drink?'

'Yes, please.'

'What would you like?'

'I don't mind.'

'I'm having mango juice. Would you like that too?'

'That sounds fine, thanks.'

'Two mango juices, coming right up.' Goliath smiled and walked to the end of the room, where a large drinks cabinet stood against the wall. He took two glasses and poured the drinks.

Tim stared at the knives and forks beside Goliath's place.

Perhaps I should steal one, he thought. A knife would allow me to protect myself.

Then he realised that the idea was ridiculous. Goliath would notice immediately that a knife was missing. He would call the guards from outside and they would disarm Tim without a struggle. A little boy – even a little boy armed with a knife – couldn't possibly fight guards armed with machine guns.

Nevertheless, stealing something seemed like a good idea. It might be useful later. Tim stretched forward and grabbed the pepper pot.

Just as Tim was stuffing the pepper pot into his pocket, Goliath turned round, carrying two glasses. Tim worried that he might have been seen, but Goliath didn't say anything. He carried the drinks to the table. 'Cheers,' said Goliath.

'Cheers.'

They clinked glasses and drank.

Goliath leaned back in his chair. He said, 'Tell me something, Tim. Are you good at general knowledge?'

'Quite,' said Tim.

'Then let me ask you a question,' said Goliath, leaning back in his chair. 'An intelligent boy like you should know the answer. What creature on this planet lives the longest?'

Tim shrugged his shoulders. He didn't have a clue. 'Humans,' he guessed.

'No, no, no. Guess again.'

'Elephants?'

'No.'

'Snakes?'

Goliath shook his head. 'The answer, as an intelligent boy like yourself should have known, is the giant tortoise. Well, a few fish have lived even longer, but who cares about fish?'

Tim was just about to answer the question – fishermen, he was going to say, and fishmongers, not to mention people who go scuba diving – but before he had a chance to speak, Goliath picked up the thread of what he had been saying.

'The giant tortoise,' said Goliath, 'is a rare and extraordinary creature which is found only in a few islands in the Indian and Pacific Oceans. Most giant tortoises live a hundred and fifty years. Some live much longer. The oldest recorded giant tortoises lived for almost three hundred years. Three whole centuries. I'll tell you a secret, Tim. I am determined to live that long too.'

Tim remembered what he had seen in the cavern. 'So you've been experimenting on them?'

'On them, yes, and their eggs. And a few other creatures too. It's been most interesting. My scientists have been feeding some creatures on a diet of tortoise eggs and others on tortoise meat. They have been injecting monkeys with tortoise blood. They have transplanted a tortoise's leg onto a rabbit and put the brain of a tortoise inside the head of a baboon. I can tell you, young man, the results have been fascinating. Every day, with the help of these animals, we are coming a little closer to the secret of eternal life.'

Tim said, 'And what about experimenting on humans?'

'Ah,' said Goliath. 'You've seen my little collection?'

'Your collection? What have you done to those people?'

'Exactly what I've done to the rabbits, the monkeys, the goats and the rats. Some of them have been injected with tortoise blood. Others eat a diet of tortoise eggs. And a few have helped with more surgical experiments, donating an ear or a kidney.'

'That's disgusting,' said Tim.

'No, no, it's not disgusting. It's just science. These creatures – and these people – are helping my scientists in their quest to discover the secret of eternal life. One or two people may have to suffer, but the whole of humanity will eventually benefit.'

Tim said, 'You can't just experiment on people!'

'Why not?'

'Because it's horrible,' said Tim. 'And it must be against the law.'

'I suppose you're probably right,' said Goliath. 'But I

141

am one of the richest men on the planet. Such petty restrictions do not concern me. Laws are for the poor.'

'No, they're not,' said Tim. 'Laws are for everyone.'

'You're very young,' said Goliath. 'You don't know much about life. Let me tell you how the world works. The rich make the laws and the poor obey them.'

Tim shook his head. 'I know enough about the world to know you shouldn't be keeping people underground in a secret laboratory. I know you shouldn't be experimenting on them. I know you can't expect to...' Midway through his sentence, Tim paused, struck by a sudden frightening thought. He said, 'Why are you telling me all this? How are you going to stop me telling the whole world what you've done here? Are you going to kill me?'

Goliath shook his head. 'No, no. I won't kill you. Not at all. I'm going to do the complete opposite.'

'What do you mean? Will you let me go?'

'Of course not,' said Goliath. 'I'm going to make you live for ever.'

'How? What will you do to me?'

'You will join my collection. My scientists will learn a lot from you. At the moment, I have some middle-aged men and women, and a few old ones, but no children. A small boy like yourself will be very useful.'

'You can't do that,' said Tim, appalled by the idea of being taken back to the cavern and confined to one of the cells. Once he was there, he was sure, he would never escape. 'You have to let me go.'

'I don't have to do anything,' said Goliath. 'This is my island. This is my kingdom. Here, I can do whatever I like.'

Tim clenched his fists. He felt furious and terrified and, worst of all, completely helpless. He said, 'My parents will come looking for me. And the police too.'

'And they'll find you,' said Goliath. 'Or rather, they'll find the remains of your boat, twenty miles from here, smashed on a rock. At this moment, my men are removing your boat from the beach and putting it into a helicopter. They'll deliver it to another island and drop it into the sea. The police are very efficient. They'll find it quickly and they'll know exactly what happened. Another stupid tourist drove his boat into a rock and drowned. They won't find your body, but that won't be any great surprise. The Indian Ocean is a vast expanse of water. They will simply assume that you were swept away by the currents and taken to the other side of the world.'

Tim stared at Goliath, speechless with horror. There was nothing he could say.

With a calm, self-satisfied smile, Goliath picked up the silver bell and rang it. Immediately, the door opened and a guard came into the room. 'Sir?'

'Could you take this young man to his cell, please.'

'Yes, sir.' The guard nodded.

Tim stared at Goliath. In a quiet voice, he said, 'You won't get away with this.'

'Oh, I will,' replied Goliath. 'That's one of the benefits of being extremely rich. When you have as much money as me, you always get away with everything.' He nodded to the guard. 'Take him away.'

Chapter 36

Four guards led Tim back along the way that he had come, marching down the stairs to the harbour and entering the underground complex. Tim was careful to watch his surroundings. If he ever got a chance to escape, he wanted to know where to go and how to find his way out.

They walked through the laboratory. The guards were vigilant and alert, watching Tim constantly, never giving him a chance to run away. Before he took two paces, they would catch him or shoot him.

At the end of a brightly-lit corridor, they reached a steel door with two buttons on the outside, a red one and a blue one. One of the guards pressed the red button. The door slid open. The other guard pushed Tim inside.

Tim stumbled into the cell. It was empty apart from a metal bucket and a white jug.

The guard drew his leg back and kicked Grk.

With a shocked squeak, Grk flew though the door and span across the floor.

The guard pressed the blue button and the door slid shut. Tim could hear the footsteps of the guards fading into the distance. And then there was silence.

Tim knew exactly what he wanted. A hot bath. Followed by a glass of cold orange juice with lots of ice. Followed by a cheese and tomato sandwich. Followed by a long snooze in his own bed.

But you can't always have what you want. Some-times, you have to be satisfied with what you've got. And this is what Tim had got: a jug of lukewarm water and a concrete floor in a damp cell.

He checked his pockets, hoping he might find a piece of chewing gum or some peanuts, but he found nothing except a pepper pot. He was depressed by his own foolishness. Why had he stolen a pepper pot? Why didn't he have the good sense to steal something useful? A sandwich, for instance, or a chicken leg. If only he'd grabbed the remnants of the picnic before abandoning his parents, he wouldn't be so hungry now.

He thought about his parents for a moment, wondering what might have happened to them. Even without a boat, he was sure that they'd have found some way to get off the island and return to the Hotel Sea Shell. By now, they'd be sitting in the hotel restaurant, tucking into a nice big supper, then heading for a long night's sleep in their comfortable beds.

Not like me, thought Tim. I don't have supper or a bed.

He drank several long glugs of water, then poured some into his cupped hand so Grk could have a drink too.

Grk licked himself all over, then walked three times in a circle and lay down. He closed his eyes and appeared to fall asleep immediately.

Tim lay down, using his own arm as a pillow, but he couldn't relax. Too many thoughts whirled through his head. He saw flashes of sights that he had seen earlier in the day, images from the island and the cavern. He remembered the creatures that he had seen confined in other cells, the tiger and the monkeys, the frightened-looking people, the tortoise with a human hand grafted onto the top of its shell. He heard the voice of Monsieur X, desperately whispering, 'Help them.' Now, finally, Tim understood what Monsieur X had meant. He knew who had to be helped.

Tim sat up. He couldn't sleep. Not now. He had to find a way to get out of here. If Monsieur X had escaped from the island, he could too.

For the first time, he took a proper look at his surroundings.

He was confined to a long, thin cell without any furniture or windows. The only light came from a yellowish bulb embedded into the ceiling.

He paced around the cell, inspecting every inch of the floor and the wall, hoping to find a loose paving stone or a hidden exit. Although he couldn't find either of those, he did discover one interesting thing. There were some markings scratched into the wall. He knelt down to inspect them more closely.

The scratches looked like letters, but he couldn't make out what they spelled.

He lay on the floor and ran his fingers along the wall. All of the scratches, he realised, made the same patterns: six upright slashes, then a seventh horizontal slash across the middle.

Immediately, Tim understood the significance of these marks. Each scratch represented a day. Each collection of seven scratches represented a week. Altogether, these scratches showed how long the cell's

146

previous occupant had stayed in here.

Had Monsieur X been here? Had these markings been made by him when he was locked in this cell? And if so, how did he manage to escape?

If Tim had wanted to depress himself even further, he could have counted up all the scratches and discovered how long he might expect to remain in this cell. But he didn't want to know that. Just by looking at the wall, he could tell already that there were hundreds of scratches, if not thousands, representing the weeks, months and years of a man's life – a life that had been wasted within these four walls.

Turning his back on the scratches, Tim sat on the floor and looked at Grk. He whispered, 'What are we going to do?'

Grk lifted his head and looked at Tim. Then he put his head down again, closed his eyes and went back to sleep.

Tim whispered, 'How can you sleep at a time like this?'

This time, Grk didn't even lift his head. He opened one eye, glanced at Tim for a moment, then closed his eye again and went back to sleep.

Tim sighed. Sometimes, he wished that Grk was a more sensible dog. Didn't he understand the urgency of their situation? Didn't he realise that they had to try and escape? Didn't he know that if they didn't find a way out of this cell and this cavern, they would have to spend the rest of their lives down here, being used by Edward Goliath's scientists in their quest to discover the secret of eternal life?

And then Tim realised that Grk was being entirely sensible. Much more sensible, in fact, than himself.

They were trapped in a small cell. The door was made of steel. The walls were solid rock. There was no way out. And so there was no point even worrying about how to escape. They shouldn't squander their energy on panic. They shouldn't waste their time getting upset or trying to think their way out of an impossible situation. Just as Grk was doing, they should sleep now and conserve their strength for tomorrow.

Tim nodded. As usual, Grk was right about everything.

Tim lay down on the concrete floor.

He whispered, 'Goodnight.' In response, Grk's tail thumped on the hard concrete floor. Then they both tried to sleep.

Chapter 37

At dusk, the blue boat chugged round the coast, heading for the jetty.

Max had his hands clasped on the wheel, steering the boat through the waves. Next to him stood Bish, his cigar clamped between his teeth, singing along to the songs on the radio. Natascha was slumped in the back of the boat, flicking through the pages of a big book filled with colourful photographs. Percy was sitting beside her, peering at the ocean through the binoculars.

It had been a long day. They were tired and hungry and very much looking forward to getting back to the hotel. Natascha wanted a long bath, filled with bubbles, followed by a quiet evening with her notebooks, writing vivid descriptions of all the extraordinary visions that she had seen at the bottom of the sea. Max wanted a large steak and lots of chips.

That afternoon, Bish had given them another lesson in diving techniques. In the afternoon, Max and Natascha had plunged off the boat, swum along a coral reef, negotiated a shoal of golden snappers, spotted a moray eel, touched an octopus and seen a hundred bewildering creatures, more colourful than anything they had believed possible.

Now, Natascha was sitting in the back of Bish's blue boat, flicking through the pages of *The Big Book of Tropical Fish*, learning the names of all the different creatures that she had seen. Max was standing at the wheel, steering the boat, completing his first lesson in how to be a sea captain.

As the blue boat rounded the final promontory and headed for the jetty, Bish looked puzzled. He stopped singing and muttered something under his breath.

Max said, 'What's wrong?'

'Look,' said Bish. He pointed at the jetty.

Max stared at the jetty. It looked completely normal. As far as he could tell, nothing had changed since this morning. 'I don't understand,' he said. 'It looks the same as when we left.'

'That's exactly the problem,' said Bish.

'What do you mean?'

'What I mean is this,' said Bish. 'Where is my boat?'

Hearing what he had said, Percy and Natascha scrambled to their feet and hurried down the cockpit to stand beside Bish and Max. All four of them stared at the jetty.

Bish was right. The jetty was empty. There was no sign of the red boat.

As soon as they reached the jetty, Max leaped from the boat and ran down to the shore, hoping to find some indication that the Malts had been here. But there was nothing.

It was getting dark. The Malts should have returned hours ago. Bish had specifically told them to leave Aubergine Island by mid-afternoon, giving themselves enough time to get home before nightfall. He didn't want them to be sailing the open seas in the dark.

Percy threw a rope to Max. 'Tie that up, please.'

Max looped the rope around one of the poles on the jetty. Natascha leaped off the boat and tied up another rope to another pole.

When the boat was secure, Bish stepped onto the jetty and shook both their hands. 'It's been a good day,' he said. 'Now, you two go back to the hotel. Who knows – they might be waiting for you there.'

Natascha said, 'Why would they be in the hotel? What about their boat?'

'They might have gone to a different jetty,' said Bish. 'Maybe they wanted to buy some souvenirs. Or watch the fishermen coming into harbour. Quite possibly, they're sitting on the terrace right now, drinking a delicious cocktail, wondering what's keeping you so long.'

Max said, 'And if they're not?'

'Then I'll see you at dawn,' said Bish. 'And we'll send out a search party.'

Natascha said, 'Can't we do that now? What if they're in trouble?'

Bish shook his head. There wasn't any point, he said. In a few minutes, the sun would set. Sending a search party into the night would just lead to more problems and more people getting lost. They would have to wait till morning.

Max and Natascha hurried back to the hotel, hoping they would find Tim, Grk and the Malts waiting in the lobby, snoozing in their rooms or sipping drinks on the terrace. But there was no sign of them.

Max quizzed the receptionist in the lobby. She

151

checked the board behind her desk and shook her head. Neither Tim nor the Malts had collected their keys. They hadn't returned to the hotel.

That night, Max and Natascha waited as long as possible, hoping the Malts would be back for supper. They got hungrier and hungrier, but they didn't want to eat alone. Max watched DVDs. Natascha sat in the hotel's library and did some research for her travel article about the Seychelles, reading books and magazines, taking lots of notes.

Eventually, they realised that the Malts weren't coming back. They sat on the hotel's terrace and shared a melancholy supper. Natascha couldn't be bothered to scold Max for eating a steak. Max didn't have the energy to tease Natascha for eating a salad. They just ate their supper, refused pudding, and went to bed, hoping that the morning would bring good news.

Chapter 38

Tim rolled over. His limbs ached. There's nothing very restful about spending a night sleeping on a hard concrete floor.

He had no idea how much time had passed. It might have been midday or midnight. The same pale yellowish glow illuminated the cell and the same strange smell wafted through the air.

The door opened. Two guards came into the room. Tim realised that he must have been woken by the sound of their footsteps in the corridor.

'Get up,' said one of the guards.

Tim said, 'Why?'

'Get up,' repeated the guard, as if he hadn't even heard Tim's question.

Slowly, reluctantly, Tim hauled himself to his feet. In a rush, he remembered the events of yesterday and what he had learnt about Edward Goliath. He remembered that this morning was the first of many, many mornings that he was condemned to spend underground, confined to this cavern.

Unless he found a way to escape.

He remembered the mournful expressions of the caged creatures on the other levels. With each day that they spent underground, they had grown more lethargic and depressed. They had given up all thought of escape. They had lost hope.

Whatever happened, he didn't want to become like them.

The two guards ushered Tim and Grk into the corridor, where three more guards were waiting. Tim was surprised. Did he really need five grown men to escort him? Who did they think he was – James Bond?

One of the guards gestured at the lead which Tim was holding in his right hand. 'Give that to me,' he said.

Tim shook his head. 'No.'

'Yes. Give it to me.'

'No,' said Tim. 'You're not taking Grk.'

'You do what I say,' insisted the guard. 'Give it to me.'

When Tim tried to protest, the guard gestured to two of his men. They stepped forward, grabbed Tim's arms and prised apart the fingers of his right hand, forcing him to release the lead.

Grk curled his lips, showing his sharp white teeth, and turned his head from side to side, threatening to bite any of the guards who came close.

One of the guards snatched the lead and jerked it violently. Grk yelped. His neck hurt. The guard jerked the lead again, even harder, and dragged Grk down the corridor. Grk tried to resist, but the guard was much stronger than him.

Every few paces, Grk turned his head, looking back. He stared mournfully at Tim. His expression was desperate. *What are they doing?* he seemed to be saying. *Where are they taking me?*

Then Grk was taken round the corner and led away.

The four guards led Tim down the stairs to the ground

floor. One marched ahead, one behind and one on either side, giving him no opportunity to escape.

Edward Goliath was talking to a group of scientists in white coats. Seeing Tim and the guards, Goliath stepped forward to greet them. 'Good morning, young man,' he said. 'Did you sleep well in your new home?'

'No,' said Tim. 'I can't sleep well on concrete.'

'You'll soon get used to it.' Goliath turned to face his scientists. 'This young man has volunteered to join our team. He has given his body to science. Later today, when I've finished showing him around our facilities, I'd like you to take all his measurements in preparation for the first experiments. Thank you, gentlemen.'

The scientists knew that they had been dismissed. They hurried in different directions around the laboratory, returning to their work.

Goliath turned his attention to Tim. 'Come with me, young man. Since this is your first day, I'm going to show you what we're doing here.'

Tim thought about protesting or refusing, but he realised that a tour of the facilities might be useful. He would be able to look for a possible escape route. He nodded and followed Goliath. The four guards walked behind them, ready to pounce if Tim tried to run away.

As they walked around the cavern, Goliath provided a running commentary, explaining the purposes of particular pieces of machinery and the roles of different people.

They passed men and women hunched over microscopes and surrounded by hundreds of test tubes filled with red, brown and black liquids. Goliath explained that they were checking how the growth and decay of blood cells could be slowed or hastened.

Goliath was proud of the facilities and pleased to have the opportunity to show a guest around. Secrecy was so important that visitors were never allowed into the cavern. He even took Tim into the control room, where screens showed images from cameras all around the facility. A huge bank of buttons and levers allowed the guards to control every aspect of life in the cavern. By pressing a button, the temperature could be raised or lowered. The door of any particular cell could be opened or shut. And so on.

There and everywhere else, Tim searched for opportunities to escape, but he couldn't see any. Cameras watched every corridor. Guards lurked beside every entrance and exit. They were all armed. If he tried to run, he wouldn't get more than five paces.

At the far end of the cavern, a hundred mice lived in small cages. Each mouse was fed a different diet and regularly checked for signs of sickness or health. Some died almost immediately. Others lived two or three times longer than mice are expected to live.

Near the mice, a giant tortoise was tethered to an enormous machine, tubes piercing its skin and shell, taking measurements all the time.

Goliath said in an excited voice, 'You see? Here it is. The secret of life. Just waiting to be discovered. As far as we can establish, this tortoise is at least two hundred and ten years old. More than two centuries. Imagine that, young man!'

Together, Goliath, Tim and the guards looked at the tortoise.

The tortoise lifted its head very slowly and turned to look at them. Its black eyes seemed to have an expression of infinite sadness.

'We're not far off,' said Goliath, his voice still humming with the same excitement. 'A few years from now – a few months, even – and we'll have cracked it. We will know why people die. We will know why people live. We will know the answer to the most important question in the world.' He leaned forward and stared at Tim. 'Tell me, young man, do you know the most important question that a human being can ask?'

'No,' said Tim.

'Think. What is the single most important question that you could ever ask?'

'I don't know.'

'Then guess. Go on, guess.'

Tim shrugged his shoulders. 'What's for lunch?'

'Very funny,' said Goliath, although he didn't laugh. 'No, I'll tell you the most important question in the world.' Goliath leaned forward and looked at Tim with a strange smile. 'The most important question in the world is this: "Why must I die?"'

When he had spoken those words, Goliath paused for a moment, waiting for a reaction, but none came. Tim just stared at him with a blank expression, trying to show none of his feelings. Goliath repeated the words again. '"Why must I die?" Have you ever asked yourself that question?'

'No,' said Tim.

'Well, you're very young,' said Goliath. 'Just wait a few years. As you get older, you will start to ask yourself that question. "Why must I die?" You will never stop asking it until the end of your life. "Why must I die?" It is the question that all human beings ask themselves. It is the question which makes us different from animals. Monkeys, dogs, dolphins – all of them are similar to humans in many ways, but none of them have the ability to ask themselves this question. It is the most important question in the world. For centuries, people have said those words. "Why must I die?" But even after these centuries, only one man has ever come close to finding an answer. And that one man is me.'

Goliath spread his arms wide to encompass everything that surrounded him – the tortoises, the mice, the scientists and all the machines and computers and cells that filled the enormous cavern.

'Here, I will discover the secret of life,' said Goliath, his eyes glittering with a strange glow. 'I will conquer death. And then I will live forever!'

For the first time, Tim realised something rather worrying. Edward Goliath wasn't just immensely rich and unbelievably powerful. He was also completely mad.

Tim said, 'You're completely mad.'

'Every genius in history has been described as a madman,' said Goliath. 'It's just one small burden that we have to bear.'

'Maybe you're not a genius,' said Tim. 'Maybe you're just completely mad.'

Ignoring what Tim had said, Goliath glanced at his watch. 'It's been fun talking to you, young man, but now

I must go. I have a very important meeting in New York. If my schedule permits, I'll be back here in a month. I look forward to seeing you then.' With a smile, Goliath turned his back on Tim and started marching away, followed by his bodyguards.

'Let me go,' cried Tim.

Goliath stopped and turned round. 'What did you say?'

'Please,' begged Tim. 'Don't keep me here. Just let me go.'

'I can't,' said Goliath.

'Why not?'

'Because you now know too much about me. I can't let you reveal what you've seen to anyone. The world won't understand what I'm trying to achieve here and they will try to stop me. I'm sorry, young man, but you've seen too much. You'll have to stay here forever.'

'I won't tell anyone,' said Tim. 'I'm good at keeping secrets.'

Goliath slowly shook his head. 'I really don't understand why you want to leave. You should be pleased to be here.'

'Pleased?' said Tim. 'Why should I be pleased?'

'By staying here and helping my scientists, think how much good you will do! Think how you will help your fellow humans! By giving your body to science, you will be benefiting the whole of humankind.'

'That's a lie,' said Tim. 'I won't be helping anyone except you.'

Goliath shook his head. 'You may think I'm selfish, but you're wrong, quite wrong. When my scientists discover the secret of eternal life, I shall not keep it to

159

myself. I shall make myself immortal, of course, but I shall allow everyone else to share the secret of immortality. Together, we will conquer death. All of us will live for ever.'

Goliath's words hung on the air for a second. Then he turned his back on Tim and walked briskly away, followed by his bodyguards.

Tim would have run after Goliath and continued begging for his freedom, but he wasn't quick enough. Before he had a chance to move, two guards grabbed his arms, one on each side, and marched him back to his cell.

Chapter 39

Grk didn't know what was happening.

He wanted to struggle, but the guard was stronger than him. Whenever Grk tried to resist, the guard tugged the lead, hurting Grk's neck.

Grk allowed himself to be led up the stairs and along the walkways. He turned his head from side to side, taking note of every interesting scent, always looking for an opportunity to escape.

On the top level of the cavern, the guard led Grk along the walkway. They passed cell after cell, then finally reached an open doorway. The guard thrust Grk inside and threw the lead after him.

Grk scampered into the small, dimly-lit cell.

The guard didn't bother removing Grk's lead. He was worried that, if he'd tried to do so, Grk would have whirled round and bitten his hand.

He was quite right to be worried. That was exactly what Grk would have done.

The guard retreated from the cell and pressed one of the buttons on the wall outside. A mesh of steel bars slid across the entrance, locking Grk inside the cell.

The guard marched away. His boots rapped against the steel walkway, growing fainter with every footstep. Then he was gone.

Everything was quiet.

Grk ran round the cell, sniffing the walls, checking

the boundaries of his new prison. It didn't take long. He was trapped inside a small, dark cell. He had a bowl of dirty water but no food. There was no blanket, no bed and, most importantly, no way out.

Grk stood in the middle of the cell, opened his mouth and howled. It was a mournful howl, a miserable howl, the type of howl that would fill you with despair. I have heard people say that no sound on earth is as terrible as the cry of a lonely dog and it's difficult to disagree with them.

Grk took a deep breath and was just about to howl again when he stopped. He turned his head to one side. His ears perked up.

He could hear a noise. He wasn't sure what it was.

He listened.

Yes, there it was again. The same noise.

It was the answering howl of another dog. And then, coming from the opposite direction, there was yet another howl.

Grk realised that the cells on either side were occupied by other dogs. He wasn't alone. He had companions.

Grk barked. The other dogs barked back again.

They couldn't see one another, but they could hear one another, and communicated by barking. The dogs interrogated Grk, asking the questions that dogs always ask of one another when they are first introduced.

Grk barked back, answering their questions and asking his own.

When he heard what they had to report, he was driven half-crazy with horror and terror. He ran round in circles, sniffing the walls of his cell all over again, hoping against hope that he might discover some way to escape, but he couldn't.

There was no way out.

If the other dogs were to be believed, Grk was going to spend the rest of his life in here, never seeing the sun, never smelling fresh air, never running on the grass, never chasing a rabbit, never doing any of the things which made a dog's life worth living.

The prospect terrified Grk. He whined and barked and howled, trying to attract Tim's attention, begging to be taken out of here, but the only responses were the whines and barks and howls of the other dogs in neighbouring cages.

Chapter 40

In the morning, Mr and Mrs Malt had started arguing as soon as they woke up and hadn't yet found any reason to stop.

They were sitting inside the shelter. It should have been a cool, calm environment. Large leaves shaded them from the piercing early morning sun. A breeze blew off the sea. But the air was hot and seemed to grow hotter with every passing minute. Patches of sweat spread across Mr Malt's shirt. Tears of frustration trickled down Mrs Malt's scarlet cheeks.

They were arguing about what to do today. Mr Malt wanted to reinforce the shelter, search the jungle for a source of clean drinking water and collect some wood for a bonfire. Mrs Malt wanted to be somewhere else. She didn't care how or where. She would have been happy to build a boat, attract the attention of a passing fisherman or even swim. She just wanted to get off the island.

Like most married couples, Mr and Mrs Malt were extremely good at arguing, particularly with one another. Mr Malt knew exactly what would upset his wife. Mrs Malt knew just how to infuriate her husband. But this morning's argument was unusually fierce and bitter. They weren't used to being so tired, so hungry and so completely stuck on a tropical island in the middle of the Indian Ocean.

'I'll tell you what's most irritating,' said Mr Malt.

'You're being so entirely illogical.'

'Me? Illogical? Hah!'

'I'm sorry, Melanie, but it's the truth. Building a boat just isn't an option. We'd be much better advised to sit tight, conserve our resources and wait to be rescued.'

'But what if we're not rescued?'

'We will be.'

'But when?'

'I don't know,' said Mr Malt. 'Today or tomorrow. Perhaps the next day.'

'I can't stay here for three days!'

'It wouldn't be the end of the world.'

'That's exactly what it would be,' said Mrs Malt. 'I need a bath. I need a cup of coffee. I need . . . ' She broke off in mid-sentence and listened for a moment. 'What's that?'

'What's what?'

'Sssh!'

They both sat very still and listened.

There was a noise like a distant lawnmower in a neighbour's garden. The noise quickly got louder. Within a few seconds, whatever was making that noise seemed to be directly overhead.

'It's an engine,' said Mrs Malt. 'Run! Or they won't know we're here!'

Mr Malt said, 'How do you know it's an engine?'

But Mrs Malt didn't bother replying. She was already scurrying through the doorway. Her elbow knocked one of the branches that held the shelter together. The structure wobbled. Mrs Malt emerged from the shelter, knocking aside another branch, and sprinted down the beach.

Behind her, the shelter creaked and shuddered. Leaves slid to the ground.

Mr Malt sprang to his feet and grabbed the roof. He was just in time to prevent the entire structure from collapsing. If he moved, the shelter would tumble to the ground. He stood there like a pillar, holding up his house with both hands.

Mrs Malt was just in time to see the helicopter soaring overhead and speeding into the distance. She stood on the beach, waving and shouting, but the pilot obviously hadn't spotted her.

'No,' moaned Mrs Malt. 'No, no, no.'

She stared in horror at the departing helicopter. It soared through the air, following the line of the beach, and curled round the island.

Mrs Malt sank to her knees on the sand. This is exactly what she'd been dreading! Their one chance to be rescued – and they'd missed it! The helicopter would never come back. They would be trapped here for days, if not weeks.

Then Mrs Malt heard a noise. Someone was shouting.

She turned her head to see who was making so much noise.

Mr Malt was standing at the top of the beach, holding a huge palm leaf in each hand. He had ripped them from the roof of his shelter. It had collapsed. But he didn't seem to care. He was waving the leaves above his head and shouting at the top of his voice. 'HERE!' he shouted. 'WE'RE OVER HERE!'

*

Staring through the windscreen, the pilot glimpsed some movement down on the beach. He couldn't see exactly what it was. He moved the controls and changed direction. The helicopter flew round the coast and came closer to investigate.

There! He could definitely see something. It looked like a man with leaves attached to both hands.

The pilot steered the helicopter down towards the shore.

As soon as the helicopter settled on the sand, four people jumped out, ducking to avoid the rotors, and ran across the beach to meet the Malts.

Max and Natascha came first, followed by Inspector Benedict and Doctor White, who was carrying an icebox and a medical bag.

The helicopter belonged to the police. Inspector Benedict had insisted on leading the search party and asked Doctor White to accompany them in case the Malts had suffered any kind of accident.

Max and Natascha took turns to hug Mr and Mrs Malt. When they had finished hugging, Doctor White quickly checked the Malts' health. He immediately realised that they were suffering from two specific ailments: dehydration and a quick temper. He reached into the icebox and pulled out the perfect cure. 'Take these,' he said, handing each of them a bottle of water and a bar of chocolate.

When the Malts had each drunk half a bottle of water and eaten several squares of chocolate, they both asked the same question. 'Where's Tim?'

'That's what we were going to ask you,' said Max.

Natascha said, 'And where's Grk?'

'We don't know,' said Mr Malt.

'Tim took the boat,' said Mrs Malt.

Inspector Benedict stared at them. 'I don't understand. Are you saying your own son deserted you on this island?'

Mr and Mrs Malt glanced at one another. Neither of them wanted to admit what Tim had done. But they knew that they must. Slowly, sadly, the Malts explained what had happened.

Inspector Benedict and Doctor White were astounded. They'd never heard of a twelve-year-old boy stealing a boat and abandoning his parents on an island. What kind of boy would do that?

Max and Natascha weren't surprised at all. They knew Tim. They knew Grk. They even had a pretty good idea why Tim and Grk would have stolen the boat and where they would have gone.

'Calypso Island,' said Max.

'We should go there now,' said Natascha. 'Before it's too late.'

'Before what's too late?' said Mrs Malt.

Natascha said, 'Before the same thing happens to him that happened to Monsieur X.'

'Or he might have gone somewhere completely different,' said Inspector Benedict. 'He might be trying to get back to Mahé. He might be drifting in the middle of the ocean. He might even be elsewhere on this island.'

Natascha shook her head. 'He'll have gone to Calypso. Something happened there. He wants to find out what.'

'We have to go there right now,' said Max. 'Before they kill him, just like they killed Monsieur X.'

Inspector Benedict reminded them that he was in command of the operation. The helicopter belonged to his police force. They would do whatever he decided. And this is what he had decided: they would search Aubergine Island first, checking for signs of any human presence, then scour the rocks for wreckage from the boat, in case Tim had smashed himself against the shore. If they couldn't find any trace of Tim, Grk or the boat on Aubergine Island, then perhaps they would fly to Calypso.

'Let's go,' said Inspector Benedict. 'We should start searching before the day gets any hotter.'

Max and Natascha glanced at one another. They knew the Inspector was making a mistake, but they also knew that there was no way to convince him of that fact. He was a responsible middle-aged man with a proper job and a smart uniform, whereas they were just a couple of kids. Reluctantly, knowing that they had failed Tim when he needed them most, Max and Natascha followed Inspector Benedict back to the helicopter.

They clambered inside and fastened themselves into their seats. The rotors spun faster. Following the Inspector's orders, the helicopter lifted into the air and headed along the line of the coast, searching the island for any sign of a boy, a dog or a boat.

Max and Natascha glanced at one another. They both knew that there was no chance of finding Tim or Grk. They were searching the wrong island.

Chapter 41

The guard paced slowly along the metal walkway, dreaming about his lunch. He didn't enjoy patrolling the cavern. It was monotonous and boring. Twice an hour, he paced the entire length of the walkways, glancing into every cell, making sure that the occupants weren't causing any trouble. They never were. If there had been any trouble, his job might have been more interesting.

When a new prisoner arrived, he or she would usually struggle for a few days. The humans would scream and shout, begging or demanding to be set free. The animals howled and growled. Some bit the bars. Others tried to dig through the walls and the floor. But they soon gave up, realising that escape was impossible. Despair sapped their strength.

The guard paused for a moment outside the tiger's cage, hoping the huge beast might lift her head and look at him, but she didn't. She was slumped on the floor, too melancholy to move.

The guard walked along the walkway, past the goats, the dogs, the rabbits and the monkeys. He hurried past the humans, then lingered near the tortoises, staring through the bars at the extraordinary creatures. He never tired of looking at them.

He walked down the staircase to the lowest level. These cells were reserved for the most recent arrivals.

He walked past a pair of pigs. He stared at the jaguar,

just delivered from China, which was pacing round and round its cage. He strolled past the newest arrival, the boy who had been placed inside his cell the previous afternoon. And then he stopped.

The guard's eyes widened.

He stepped closer to the bars and stared into the cell.

The boy was lying on the ground. He wasn't moving. He didn't even appear to be breathing.

The guard panicked. He didn't know what to do.

If the boy was dead...

If the boy was dead, the guard knew exactly what would happen. He would be killed too. Edward Goliath paid great rewards for good work, but he inflicted terrible punishments for bad work.

The guard stood there for a few more seconds, hoping against hope that the boy would roll over or sneeze or show some signs of life, but he just lay there, not moving, not breathing, apparently dead.

There was only one thing to do. The guard pressed the blue button. The bars slid open.

The guard wasn't stupid. He knew that prisoners play tricks. But he had already seen this boy for himself. He wasn't big enough or strong enough to cause a threat. He wouldn't be able to hurt anyone.

The guard stepped into the cell. He said, 'Boy?'

There was no response.

He spoke a bit louder. 'Hey, boy!'

There was still no response.

The guard knelt on the cold concrete floor and put his hand on the boy's shoulder. He said, 'Boy! What's wrong with you?'

171

Still, the boy didn't answer.

The guard leaned forward and said, 'Come on, boy, what's going on? Can you hear me?'

There was a sudden movement, so fast that it seemed like a blur.

The guard didn't even have time to react. He just felt a terrible pain in his eyes and nose. He grabbed his face, screaming, and fell to the ground.

Tim waited until the last possible moment. He knew he would have only one chance. He was small, thin and weak. In a fair fight, he couldn't possibly defeat a grown man. He wouldn't even survive one punch.

He waited, not moving, trying not to breathe, until he could feel the guard looming over him.

From the sound of the guard's voice, Tim guessed where the guard's face must be. He hoped he was right. If he was wrong...It wasn't even worth thinking about what would happen if he was wrong.

He waited until the last possible moment, then he whirled round, raised his right hand and hurled the contents of the pepper pot into the guard's face.

The guard scrabbled desperately at his eyes, trying to scrape away the source of the pain. His lips throbbed. His nostrils stung as if they'd been bitten by fifty wasps. His eyes dribbled tears.

And then he remembered the boy.

He rolled over on the ground, reaching for the boy with both hands, grabbing at the air, determined to get his revenge.

But Tim was too quick. He dodged away from the guard's swirling arms, sprang to his feet and ran for the door. Before the guard could even start to react to the sound of his footsteps, Tim had sprinted through the open doorway and started running down the metal walkway.

Behind him, he could hear a roar of anguish and fury. The guard shouted for help. It would only take a few seconds for his colleagues to realise that something was wrong.

Tim ran round the walkway. He sprinted past cells containing dogs, tortoises and people, turning his head quickly to glance into each one, but there was no sign of Grk. He ducked behind a stack of computers and stopped, panting, trying to decide what to do next.

He looked around. He was hidden behind a tall bank of electronic equipment. Wires trailed across the floor. He could hear shouts and footsteps. The guard must have alerted his colleagues.

Tim tried to think how he could escape from the cavern. He had to reach an exit and take a lift to the surface. Then, he would have to get off the island and find help. If he managed to contact the police, they could come back to Calypso and see for themselves what Edward Goliath had done.

But how could he get off the island?

How could he even get out of the cavern, let alone find a way to cross the ocean?

It's hopeless, thought Tim. I might as well give up now.

He sighed.

I'll never get out of here alive, he thought. And even

if I do, I'll never get off the island.

He sighed again.

And then he remembered the tortoises.

He thought of the first giant tortoise that he had seen, the one that he had mistaken for a green rock. He remembered how Grk had run across the clearing.

I'm not going to give up now, thought Tim. I have to find a way out of here. I have to rescue the giant tortoises and stop Edward Goliath experimenting on them.

He turned to the left, then the right, searching his surroundings, trying to decide which way to go.

To the right, there was a line of cages, packed with mice and rats. To the left, just a few paces away, there was a doorway that he recognised. It led into the control room.

Tim had an idea.

He smiled. Yes, he thought. That's a pretty good idea.

He hurried to the doorway and glanced inside. The control room was empty. The guards must have gone to help their colleagues. He went into the room.

He stared at the panel which controlled every aspect of life inside the cavern. There must have been a hundred buttons and levers of different shapes, sizes and colours. None of them was marked. Tim had no idea which did what. Some must have opened doors. Others must have controlled the lights, the temperature, the flow of hot and cold air.

Given more time, Tim could have taken a scientific approach, pressing each button in turn, checking what happened, but he didn't have time to be sensible or rational. He knew that the guards would be here any minute. Reinforcements must already be coming down from the surface.

Working his way from one end of the panel to the other, he pressed every button and pulled every lever.

For a moment, nothing happened.

Then there was chaos.

The panel lit up. Dials flickered. A siren sounded, then another and then a third, all of them shrieking at top volume.

Tim put his hands over his ears. The noise was unbearable. He hurried to the door and looked at the cavern.

There, the chaos was even more extraordinary. Bulbs flickered on and off. Doors opened and shut. Water gushed through pipes. Air fizzed through tubes. The air was filled with a cacophony of extraordinary sounds, getting louder with every passing second – footsteps, shouts, barking, yells, a gunshot, a piercing scream, the roar of metal, the screech of steel, all jumbled together.

Every cell had opened. Every animal had been set free.

Some of them were so depressed, weak or tired that they couldn't bring themselves to move. They just sat in their cells, staring at the open doorway, wondering what had happened to the steel bars, not bothering to escape.

But others ran.

Dogs dashed along the metal walkways. Rats scampered up and down the stairs. Monkeys swung from platform to platform. Goats wandered across the floor, stopping to chew on computer wires or chomp through a sheaf of papers.

And wherever you looked, there were mice. Brown mice and white mice, big mice and small mice, fat mice and thin mice, dancing on the computers, paddling through the pools of water, disappearing down corridors, searching every part of the cavern. Some of the mice had spent their entire lives inside a tiny little cage. Now, for the first time, they were tasting freedom.

Guards and scientists sprinted across the floor and along the walkways. The guards were trying to impose order, firing shots into the air, forcing animals and prisoners back into the cells. The scientists were trying to save their research. Some pulled computers away from gushing streams of water. Others slammed the doors of cages to stop mice escaping. None of them had time to notice a boy, standing in a darkened doorway, watching the chaos with a quiet smile on his face.

Tim turned his head from side to side, looking for a route through the confusion, trying to decide which way to run.

And then he frowned.

He had realised that he couldn't get out of here. Not yet. Not alone. First, he had to find Grk.

Tim took a couple of paces into the cavern and peered upwards at the metal walkways, searching for any sign of a small black and white dog.

Chapter 42

The tiger opened her eyes and lifted her head. She could hear strange noises. She could smell unexpected scents. Something had changed.

At the edge of her vision, she glimpsed some movement.

She turned her head and looked through the doorway.

There was a goat standing in the corridor. It stared at her, then bleated twice and padded away.

The tiger blinked. She noticed that something had changed. There were usually big steel bars blocking the doorway, preventing her from leaving, protecting anyone who came down the corridor to bring her food or inspect her, but the bars had gone. Her cell had no door. If she wanted to leave, she could walk out now.

She laid her head on the concrete again.

For more than a year now, she had been confined to this cell. She had been captured in the jungle by a hunter and sold to Edward Goliath, then put in a crate and transported to Calypso Island by ship and helicopter. For a year, she had seen nothing but these walls and the people who walked down the corridor past her cell. Every day at the same time, her meal was delivered. Day by day, she had lost any enthusiasm for life.

She ate and slept and lay on the concrete. That was her life. Eating, sleeping, dozing, doing nothing. When she was first confined in this cell, she used to pace round and round in circles, walking miles every day, but she had eventually stopped even doing that. Now, she just lay on the floor and dozed. Day by day, week by week, she had forgotten the jungle, her home. She had forgotten how to hunt and how to run.

There was another movement in the corridor. A white mouse ran along the floor, its nose wrinkling, sniffing. The mouse was followed by another, then two more, and then a dog which glanced through the open doorway at the tiger, growled briefly and hurried away.

Deep in the tiger's memory, a vision stirred. A memory of chasing animals through the jungle. She remembered catching her own food, sprinting through the trees, wading through rivers, clambering up mountains and plunging down valleys.

It had felt good. She remembered that now.

She hauled herself to her feet and took a few unsteady steps towards the open doorway.

Chapter 43

One of the guards called the mansion and spoke to Toby Connaught, explaining that the prisoners had escaped. Toby Connaught alerted the rest of the guards, ordering reinforcements to proceed immediately to the cavern, then left the mansion and ran across the grass to the helicopters.

On the lawn, Edward Goliath's helicopter was ready to take off.

Goliath was standing on the grass, discussing a few final preparations with the mechanics. They had been making some modifications to his helicopter, shedding some spare weight, making it even faster.

Toby Connaught interrupted their conversation to explain what had happened.

Goliath did not take the news well. His face turned bright red with fury. He cancelled his helicopter flight. 'I'm not going to leave the island until that boy has been caught,' he said, 'even if I have to catch him myself.'

Tim stood in the open doorway, wondering what to do.

He didn't know which way to turn. He didn't know whether to climb up the stairs or run round the walls or stay here, hoping to see some sign of Grk.

He watched the scene of chaos swiftly engulfing the cavern. In just a few seconds, a calm and secure scientific laboratory had been turned into a jungle, running with wild beasts. All the doors had opened. Every prisoner had been set free.

The cavern was packed with noise and movement. Mice charged across the computers. Dogs chased rats along the walkways. Goats chewed wires. Monkeys swung down the stairways. A giant tortoise slowly lifted its enormous head and peered at the chaos with big black eyes.

But there was no sign of Grk.

The doors opened. Four guards emerged from the lift and started running. They sprinted down the corridor, emerged through the open door and ran along the walkway.

Each of the guards was armed with a machine gun. They had been issued with strict orders. They knew exactly what they were looking for. They turned their heads from side to side, searching for the boy.

Find him, Toby Connaught had said. Whatever you do, find him. I want that boy. Dead or alive, I don't care. Just get the boy.

The guards ran fast.

They charged down the staircase and ran along the next level. They had a routine. One by one, they checked every cell, making sure it was empty. They found no sign of the boy.

And then, just before they checked the last cell on the level, all four guards stopped.

Right ahead of them, there was a tiger.

They could have lifted their guns, pulled the triggers and shot the tiger. But they were too shocked to move.

They just stood there, mouths wide open, hands hanging by their sides, staring in astonishment.

The tiger took advantage of their indecision. With a roar, she leaped through the air. Chasing goats was fun. Chasing dogs was fun too. But chasing humans – that was what she really wanted to do.

Humans had snatched her from the jungle, transported her across the sea and locked her in this dungeon. She hated humans.

Her mouth open, her sharp white teeth dripping saliva, she sprinted down the walkway.

The four guards dropped their guns and ran.

Not for the first time, Tim wondered whether dogs were cleverer than humans.

He had been standing in the doorway, trying to think of some way to find Grk. He had stared around the cavern, observing the signs of chaos and destruction, feeling scared and lonely and completely helpless. He had even wondered whether to escape alone and save himself, hoping that Grk would find his own way out.

He had looked left and then right and then left again, trying to imagine what was the best course of action and soon realising that he didn't have a clue what to do.

And then Grk just appeared.

He sprinted across the floor and threw himself into Tim's arms.

Grk stuck out his tongue and licked Tim's face, covering his lips and cheeks and nose with doggy saliva.

'Uhh,' said Tim, giggling. 'Stop! Stop! That tickles!'

But he didn't push Grk away.

Somehow, Grk had known how and where to find Tim. He had negotiated the stairways and the walkways. He had dodged the guards and the prisoners. And, best of all, he had known where to go. While Tim had stood in this doorway, helpless and bewildered, Grk had somehow managed to find him.

Dogs were definitely cleverer than humans.

Tim put Grk on the ground. He wiped his face with his sleeve. He said, 'Let's get out of here. Okay?'

Grk looked up at Tim, barked twice and wagged his tail.

Tim took that to mean 'yes'.

Together, Tim and Grk ran across the cavern's floor.

Chapter 44

In the barracks, six guards were lounging around, playing cards, when the siren sounded. They sprang to their feet and grabbed their guns.

The radio buzzed, giving them a simple order. *Get down to the cavern! Find the boy! Now!*

They ran out of the barracks. On the other side of the harbour, they clambered aboard the wagon and whizzed straight down the tracks to the cavern.

At the end of the tracks, the wagon stopped. The guards jumped out. The door swung open. The six guards poured into the cavern, their guns raised, ready to shoot...

...and then they just stood there, their mouths open, their eyes blinking in amazement, unable to believe the scene of chaos that confronted them.

None of them turned round. None of them noticed what was happening behind them. Which was why none of them saw a small boy and a dog creeping along the wall, sneaking through the doors and clambering inside the wagon.

Tim pressed the button. The wagon shot along the track.

Tim and Grk sat on the wooden bench and watched the walls flashing past.

When they reached the end of the tunnel, two doors slid open automatically. The wagon whooshed out of the tunnel and sped down the quay. Under the wheels, a switch clicked, disabling the current. The wagon rolled slowly to a halt.

As soon as the wheels stopped turning, Tim jumped out, followed by Grk. They sprinted round the harbour.

The sun had risen in the sky and the air was hot. After a few paces, Tim was sweating and Grk was panting.

Moored in the harbour, just as Tim had remembered from his previous visit, there were six powerful speedboats, a pair of small yachts and a massive white cruiser, *The Fountain of Youth*.

Several sailors were working on the cruiser's deck, polishing brass and coiling ropes. None of them noticed Tim or Grk.

Tim would have preferred to board the biggest speedboat, because it would go fastest, but he was worried that he wouldn't know how to start its engine. Instead, he ran round the quay to a small speedboat which looked quite similar to Bish's boat.

Tim sprang between the shore and the boat. Grk followed him. They jumped into the cabin. Staring at the dials and levers, Tim was relieved to see that the controls were just about the same as the controls in Bish's boat. Even better, the key was sitting in the ignition.

The speedboat was attached to the quay by two ropes, looped around cleats at its bow and stern. Tim unlooped the ropes and let them drop into the water. He jumped back into the cabin and turned the key. The engine coughed, coughed again, then spluttered into life.

Now, thought Tim, I have to remember exactly what to do.

He nudged the throttle. The engine snarled.

He pulled the throttle further downwards. The engine roared and the boat zoomed forward. The hull banged against the boat on the left, leaving a dent, and banged again against the boat on the right, leaving another dent, then sped out of the harbour, leaving a foamy white wake on the surface of the water.

On the deck of *The Fountain of Youth*, a couple of the sailors turned round, alerted by the sound of the engine. They peered across the harbour. For a moment, neither of them could believe what they were seeing. Then, one of the sailors ran to fetch his boss and the other shouted at Tim, ordering him to stop.

Over the noise of the engine, Tim couldn't hear what the sailor was shouting. Even if he had been able to hear, he wouldn't have cared. He had more important things to worry about.

Tim pulled the throttle as far as it would go.

The engine churned the waves, spitting foam. The boat leaped forward, cutting through the water. The strong wind swept over Tim, almost blowing the hairs off his head, and grabbed at Grk, threatening to pick him up and throw him out of the cabin.

Tim knew he didn't have much time. They would soon be coming after him. He turned the front of the boat to face the open water and headed away from Calypso.

As the boat emerged from the protection of the harbour, the waves grew larger. The boat was thrown from side to side. Tim clung to the steering wheel. Grk staggered from one side of the cabin to the other, desperately trying to keep his balance.

The ocean stretched ahead of them, vast and empty. On the horizon, Tim could see a few slim dark shapes. He hoped they were the nearest islands. He turned the wheel and pointed the boat towards the island which looked nearest.

Edward Goliath sprinted across the lawn.

The mechanics were preparing the helicopters, the pilots were huddled in a group and several guards had assembled, carrying their weapons, but no one was actually doing anything. Every minute, the boy in the boat was getting further away from the island, but no one was making any effort to stop him.

There was an old English saying that Goliath had always liked. He'd heard it for the first time about fifty years ago, spoken by a teacher at his school, and it had lodged in his brain. In the fifty years since then, he had probably spoken those nine words to himself almost every day.

If you want something done right, do it yourself.

That's absolutely true, thought Goliath. It was true fifty years ago and it's still true today.

He clicked his fingers at one of his guards. 'Give me that.' He pointed at the guard's machine gun.

The guard stared at him, speechless with surprise.

'Come on, come on,' said Goliath. 'Give it to me!'

'Yes, sir.'

The guard lifted the strap over his head and handed the gun to Goliath.

Goliath grabbed the gun and ran across the grass to his helicopter. He clambered inside, put the headphones over his ears and tucked the machine gun between his feet.

A minute later, the helicopter was airborne and heading towards the ocean.

If you want something done right, thought Goliath, do it yourself.

A wave crashed against the side of the boat, sending a cold spray into the cabin, soaking Tim and Grk.

Grk yelped. He wasn't having fun. He was cold, wet and seasick. He scampered to the back of the cabin.

Tim wasn't having fun either. He was cold, wet, seasick and scared.

He gripped the steering wheel with both hands, using all his strength to keep the boat facing forwards.

He was struggling to control the boat. The wind and the water were his enemies. They used every tactic to disarm and disable him. They bashed him and nudged him, spat at him and soaked him, slapped him and shoved him.

Water foamed in the bottom of the cabin. Tim wanted to scoop it overboard with a bucket, but he didn't dare let go of the wheel.

Once more, he glanced behind, looking back the way that he had come.

The island was shrinking quickly. His was still the only boat in the sea. Perhaps he wouldn't be followed. Perhaps he was free.

And then, from the top of the island, he saw a small speck lifting into the air. From here, it looked no bigger than a mosquito.

With each second, the speck grew larger.

Tim felt a sudden rush of terror. He knew exactly what the speck was.

He turned and faced forwards. The ocean was ahead of him. The nearest island looked no closer. He'd never reach it in time.

Tim pulled the throttle, hoping against hope that the engine would release more power, and steered towards the horizon.

Tim looked over his shoulder once more. The speck was bigger now. It was approaching fast. In a minute or two, it would be overhead.

He didn't know what to do.

He couldn't outrun a helicopter. The boat was too slow.

He couldn't hide. He and Grk were standing in an open boat, floating in the middle of the ocean. They were completely exposed.

What could he do?

Chapter 45

Over the noise of the boat's engine, Tim could hear another noise, a fierce humming. It sounded like a fly buzzing against a windowpane, trying to get out of the house.

Tim knew what that noise meant. He looked up.

The helicopter was swooping through the sky, heading directly towards the boat. It was so close that Tim could clearly distinguish every detail of the undercarriage.

Through the helicopter's open door, Tim could see the pilot, hunched over the controls. Even from this distance, he recognised Edward Goliath.

Goliath held the helicopter steady with one hand and reached down with his other hand. He removed something that had been lying beside his feet. Something that looked like a walking stick. As the helicopter swept overheard, Goliath poked the stick out of the window and pointed it at the boat.

A burst of gunfire came from above. Tim threw himself down and rolled across the cabin. Bullets splattered through the water and along the deck. A line of holes appeared in the deck.

The wheel spun. The boat rolled helplessly from side to side. Foam and spray fizzed through the air and splashed into the cabin, covering Tim with water, soaking him completely.

If he stayed like this, Tim realised, he didn't have a chance. He jumped up, ran across the cabin and grabbed the wheel. He tried to control the boat. Then he realised that something was missing. No – not something – someone. Where was Grk?

Tim turned round. He looked up and down the cabin. To his horror, he realised he was alone.

Grk had disappeared.

Had he been swept overboard?

Tim let go of the wheel and ran to the side of the boat. He stared at the ocean, searching the huge waves, but he couldn't see any sign of a small black and white dog. He ran to the other side of the boat, but he couldn't see Grk there either.

Where had he gone?

Tim shouted, 'GRK!'

The only response was the buzzing of the helicopter's rotors. He looked up. Goliath had wheeled through the air and was coming back for a second shot at the boat.

Tim shouted, 'GRK!'

Woof woof!

Tim turned round. What was that noise? Was that just the sound of the waves crashing against the side of the boat?

Woof woof!

Yes – there it was again. He'd heard something. He was sure he had. The sound of a dog, barking for help. But where was it coming from? The sea? The waves? Which direction?

Woof woof!

This time, Tim heard exactly where the noise was coming from. He ran to the stern of the boat and dropped down to the deck.

190

Grk had crawled into a cupboard at the back of the cabin. He was lying on a pile of red cushions, shivering. He lifted his head and stared at Tim. It was quite obvious from his expression that Grk was cold, cross and seasick, and he wanted to go home.

'I'm really sorry,' said Tim. 'But I don't know if we're ever going to go home.'

Grk barked. *Woof woof!*

Tim said, 'What's that supposed to mean?'

Grk barked again. *Woof woof!*

Tim said, 'I don't know what you're trying to say.'

Grk barked a third time. *Woof woof!*

Behind Grk, nestling among the cushions, Tim saw three red tubes. When he realised what they were, his eyes widened. 'You're a genius,' said Tim. 'Grk – you are a genius.'

Chapter 46

The helicopter flew lower and lower, barely skimming the surface of the waves. Goliath aimed the gun at the boat, preparing to fire. This time, he was determined to hit the boy. This time, he would not miss. 'If you want something done right,' he whispered to himself, 'do it yourself.' His finger tightened on the trigger.

As the helicopter approached, Tim stood in the middle of the boat, his feet apart, and pointed the red flare into the sky. It had a simple design. You held the body of the flare in one hand and pulled a short cord with the other.

He wasn't quite sure what would happen when he pulled the cord. The flare might explode or ignite. He might blow his hand off or lose an eye.

But even losing an eye is better than being shot by a madman with a machine gun.

Tim aimed the flare at the helicopter's cabin, hoping it would smack against the rotors or smash the windscreen, forcing Goliath to turn round and return to the island.

The helicopter came closer and closer.

Tim forced himself to wait until the last possible moment. He stayed standing still, a completely exposed target, until the helicopter was directly overhead. Then he pulled the cord.

There was a fizz and a bang. The flare shot into the

air, leaving a trail of smoke. It missed the helicopter, continued up, up, up into the sky and exploded in a frothing ball of bright red smoke.

Inside the helicopter, Goliath panicked.

He didn't understand what had happened. Did the boy have a bazooka? A rocket launcher? A mortar? He pulled the helicopter upwards, away from the boat, and circled back towards the island, putting a safe distance between himself and the boy.

He glanced back, checking that he wasn't being attacked again, and saw a trail of red smoke stretching into the sky. Immediately, he understood what it was.

Goliath laughed. He was impressed. The boy wasn't an idiot. Firing a flare – that was a clever idea.

Clever, but not clever enough.

Goliath turned the helicopter around and prepared for a second attack.

Max was the only person to see it. He shouted, 'What was that?'

He was sitting in the police helicopter with Natascha, Mr and Mrs Malt, Inspector Benedict, Doctor White and the pilot. Over the noise of the engine, no one had heard what he said. He tugged Natascha's sleeve and shouted louder. 'DID YOU SEE THAT?'

She shouted back, 'DID I SEE WHAT?'

'THAT!' He pointed through the window.

Natascha turned and stared. Through the helicopter's window, she could see the distant tiny trail of red smoke fading into the sky. It must have been several miles away. She shouted, 'WHAT'S THAT?'

'I DON'T KNOW,' shouted Max. He looked around the helicopter. No one else had seen the smoke. They were too busy staring down at Aubergine Island, searching the trees and the rocks for any sign of a boy, a dog or a boat.

Tim grabbed another flare.

The helicopter swooped over the waves. Tim stared upwards, watching the rotors and the shape of Goliath, hunched over the controls. He could clearly see the black machine gun in Goliath's hand.

The end of the gun crackled with bright light. There was a rattle of explosions. Bullets smacked into the boat, puncturing fibreglass and metal, sending sparks in every direction.

Tim waited, trying not to panic, letting the helicopter come closer and closer and closer. When he couldn't wait another second, he pulled the cord.

The flare spat and roared and shot into the air, leaving a trail of smoke. It missed the helicopter, whizzed up, up, up into the sky, even higher than the first, and exploded in another cloud of scarlet smoke.

This time, Max and Natascha were waiting for the flare.

As soon as the red smoke exploded in the sky, they shouted to the others, drawing their attention to it.

The Malts turned round. So did Inspector Benedict. Everyone realised immediately what the flare meant. Someone was in trouble – and perhaps that someone was Tim.

Inspector Benedict issued a quick order to the pilot. The helicopter curled through the air, changing direction, leaving the island and heading across the ocean towards the source of the flare.

Goliath smiled. He was enjoying himself.

The life of a billionaire is often boring.

Meetings. Lunches. Dinners. Flying from New York to Tokyo to Sydney to London and then back to New York again. Oh, it might sound glamorous, but it's actually exhausting and irritating and quite dull.

This was much more fun.

He readied the machine gun. Down below, he could see the boat bobbing on the water and the two small figures inside the cabin, the boy and the dog, their little faces lifted, staring at the sky. In his right hand, the boy was holding another flare.

Goliath admired the boy's spirit. He liked someone who fought back. A pity, thought Goliath, that I'm going to have to kill him.

He eased the controls forward and swooped across the ocean.

There was one flare left. It was his last chance.

When the final flare was gone, Tim had decided, he would throw himself overboard. He didn't want to wait here like a condemned man in front of a firing squad. He would plunge into the sea, holding Grk in his arms, and try to stay afloat. He might drown or get eaten by sharks, but that was better than sitting here in this boat, a sitting target, being shot to pieces.

He held the the flare in his right hand and the cord in his left. He waited for the helicopter to come closer. He tried to ignore all the other sounds and sensations – the roaring engines, the buzzing rotors, the cold, the wet, the waves throwing the boat from side to side – and concentrated on the helicopter.

This is it, thought Tim. This is my last chance.

He pulled the cord.

Chapter 47

The flare fizzed through the air.

It flew straight into the helicopter, banged against a strut behind the pilot's seat and exploded.

Scarlet smoke filled the interior of the helicopter.

Goliath couldn't see. He could hardly breathe.

He wrestled with the controls. The helicopter lurched and plunged like a wild horse trying to throw a rider off its back.

Goliath dropped the gun. It slid across the floor, fell out of the helicopter and tumbled through the air. There was a small splash. Then the gun was gone, sinking down to the bottom of the sea.

Goliath didn't even notice. He had too many other things to worry about. His eyes stung. His lungs ached. He didn't know where he was going or what he was doing.

The helicopter flew to the left, then the right, lurching desperately from one side to the other, soaring into the air, then plunging down towards the sea.

Through the smoke, Goliath could suddenly see the ocean rushing towards him. He pulled the controls violently. The helicopter twisted and shuddered and almost managed to lift into the air again, but a rotor on the tail – just a single rotor – scraped the foaming crest of a wave and snapped off.

The removal of that one rotor was enough to condemn

the helicopter. The entire machine swivelled and tipped over and collapsed into the sea.

The windscreen smashed. All the rotors shattered. Sparks flew. Metal crunched. Like a mosquito slapped by a man's palm, the helicopter crumpled into the water.

Goliath screamed and struggled with his seatbelt, trying to free himself.

The fuel tank cracked open. Liquid spilled out.

As soon as the fuel met a spark, there was a loud bang and a huge ball of orange flame lifted into the air.

A great gust of heat flashed across the water, knocking Tim and Grk backwards, throwing them from one end of the cabin to the other.

They lay there for a second, stunned.

Wave after wave struck the side of the boat.

Grk rolled over and licked his burnt fur.

Tim touched his singed eyebrows and scorched skin. His face felt as if he'd been lying in the sun all day.

He sat up and peered over the side of the boat.

He saw flaming oil and black smoke and, in the midst of the burning wreckage, a human body, floating face down in the water.

Chapter 48

Six days after the death of Edward Goliath, a blue boat chugged across the ocean.

Four people were inside the boat. Four people and a small dog.

Bish stood at the wheel, a cigar clamped between his teeth, clouds of grey smoke surrounding his face. Max and Natascha and Tim sat in the cabin, taking turns to peer at the ocean through the binoculars, searching for whales. Grk lay at their feet, dozing.

Mr and Mrs Malt had decided to stay in the hotel and spend the day beside the pool, reading their books.

When the boat reached Calypso, Bish moored against the quay. He told the children to go ahead without him. He was going to stay in his boat, he explained. When the three children had jumped ashore, followed by Grk, Bish stretched out in the shade, pulled his cap over his face and fell asleep.

Together, the three children walked round the quay and clambered up the steps that led from the harbour to the mansion. Grk stopped to sniff a fishy-smelling bucket, then hurried after them.

At the top of the steps, they found the road and walked slowly towards the centre of the island. They had been walking for ten or fifteen minutes when Tim pointed and said, 'There! Look! Do you see?'

The others stopped and looked.

Natascha said, 'What are we supposed to be looking at?'

'That,' said Tim.

'What?'

'The thing that looks like a green rock.'

Grk bounded ahead, his tail wagging, and barked loudly. *Woof woof! Woof woof woof!* Surprised by the noise, the giant tortoise slowly lifted its head.

Tim, Max and Natascha gathered round, looking at the giant tortoise, inspecting its big head and its black eyes and its plump feet and its enormous shell.

The tortoises were safe now.

The police had emptied Goliath's laboratories. His prisoners were taken to hospitals and zoos. The tortoises stayed behind. There was no reason for them to leave the island.

Goliath had never made a will, because he hadn't believed that he was ever going to die. His six ex-wives, seven children and nine grandchildren were going to spend the next few decades suing one another to decide how to divide all his money. The government of the Seychelles had decided to take control of Calypso until the lawsuits finished and convert the island into a nature reserve.

It's always impossible to predict the future. Anything might happen. A tidal wave might sweep the Seychelles away. The seas might rise so high that all the islands are submerged. Thousands of miles away, a pair of idiotic politicians might decide to have a war and destroy the entire planet with their bombs.

But let's hope Calypso is spared these or any other

disasters. And then, with a bit of luck, the giant tortoises will be able to continue living peacefully on the island for a long, long time.